DOPE BOY DREAMS

DOPE BOY DREAMS

By Antonio Roundtree

Published by
MIDNIGHT EXPRESS BOOKS

DOPE BOY DREAMS

Copyright © 2013 by Antonio Roundtree

ISBN-13   978-0-9888063-1-3
ISBN-10   0988806312

Disclaimer: This is a work of fiction. All characters are totally from the imagination of the author and depict no persons, living or dead; any similarity is totally coincidental.

Published by
MIDNIGHT EXPRESS BOOKS
POBox 69
Berryville AR 72616
(870) 210-3772
MEBooks1@yahoo.com

DOPE BOY DREAMS

By Antonio Roundtree

CHAPTER 1

DAY 1

THE BEGINNING

The big yellow school bus pulled up to the bus stop. This was Omar's first day in the new school. His mom had worked hard to purchase the used brick house several miles outside the city limits. Omar cried like a baby when she drove him there the first time to show him his new home. Omar hated the fact that he would be so far away from the little homies he had grown up with and knew from the surroundings that this place was too boring. There was nothing around and the closest store was a little over a mile away. There was no game room, recreation center or swimming pools or nothing the inner-city had to offer. There was nothing but trees, three bedroom brick homes and farm land. Omar was sick.

A month or two into his stay in the burbs, Omar put his fight-game down on a few of the country boys, so his name spread quickly around the country.

Omar was real nice with his hands. Everyone admired his $300 white-diamond bike. Everybody admired so. Omar was the shit; a new face was always good in the country. Plus, he was from the city, so his respect level was high.

As Omar made his way down the isle of the bus, a few kids whispered and made comments on the fresh pair of Troops and matching sweat suit he had on. Not too far behind Omar was his new homie, Tight. The only friend he could see himself hanging with since he'd moved to the country.

As Omar took a seat in the very back of the bus, he noticed the prettiest little thing he'd seen since he moved to the country. She wore a mushroom hair-do with long black hair hanging halfway down her back. Their eyes met and he knew he had to have her.

The bus pulled into the school yard, so Omar made his move. The girl's name was Tonya and she already knew about his reputation and wanted to kick it with him. So, within minutes, Omar was writing down her phone number; he was very pleased.

As the school day progressed, Omar raised his hand to be excused to use the restroom. On the way down the hall, he bumped into Julita, his big brother's baby momma's sister, and they kicked it a few minutes.

Out of the blue, Julita asked him if he wanted some weed.

Omar didn't smoke, but said yeah because he figured Tight would be glad to get it; he had seen Tight and a few other boys smoke.

Julita told him to follow her into the bathroom.

Omar watched as she reached inside of her jean jacket. He expected her to pull out a dime bag, but instead, she pulls out a half a pound of some dodo-brown and gave it to him. She said, "Here, O; you can have it."

Not really knowing its value, he knew it was more than he'd ever seen in his 13 years of living. Omar snatched the bag and put it in his jacket and got back to class telling Julita he would call her.

Back in class, his mind raced as he watched the clock ready for 3 o'clock, so he could show Tight what he had.

On the bus ride home, Tight and Omar discussed how to get rid of the brown seedy-ass weed. Tight told O that everybody in the boring-ass country smoked weed; shit, there wasn't anything else to do. They could make a killing selling the weed at school. So that night, they sat in O's room rolling joints. Tight offered to sell as many as he could the next day in school.

The following day was a big success. Tight sold 15 joints and brought Omar $15; back in '86, joints were a dollar a piece. O didn't know it then, but his life was about to change; big time.

That night two white boys came and picked Tight up in their father's BMW with hopes of scoring 2 ounces of weed for $200. Tight had them drive around the corner to Omar's house to make the buy.

Omar's mom grew suspicious when she noticed the big 735i with two white boys in it pull into her driveway, but brushed it off when she seen Tight, Omar's new friend from the neighborhood.

Tight went in the house and told O to go to his bedroom so they could speak in private. Omar went in the bedroom and asked Tight who was in the BMW. Tight told him that the white boys were in his class and had a rich father and they wanted to buy two ounces.

The white boys even brought along a digital scale to weigh the bud. Omar didn't have a clue, but watched closely as Tight weighed two ounces and rushed out to get the money.

When he returned, he handed Omar two crisp $100 bills.

Omar quickly wrapped the two C-notes around the 15 ones that he had made earlier at school, and a feeling of power instantly came over him.

Omar ended up selling all the weed, coming up with about $900. After fronting in the lunch line every day like he was big time, the word quickly spread that O and Tight were getting money.

Two months later, O rolled off the top of Tonya, who he had nicknamed Papoose.

Omar's mom was working a second shift and he had just finished fucking Papoose's tight wet pussy. It was good to O. He just happened to be the 3rd nigga to taste her young tight sweetness.

About that time, Omar's new homeboy Tone, from New York had just whipped his 85 Nissan Max into his driveway with good news. He showed O a hand full of little pieces of rock that looked like chipped off pieces of soap. He said, "My nigga, this is what everybody wants. Come down Nash Street and I'll show you."

As they entered the 500 block of East Nash Street, fiends were everywhere buying crack.

A few crack dealers knew O for having weed.

By now, Omar had fucked Julita good and brought her some Reebok classics so she stole a pound a week from her dad who owned a few night clubs and sold so much weed it took him a few months to catch on that his shit was coming up short.

By then Omar had a new idea. O paged Jamfackin Slick, a guy he was introduced to by Tone. When the phone rang in the phone booth O told Slick to meet him at the fish and chip shop on the corner of the 500 block.

When Slick arrived in his purple 190E, Omar hopped in and informed Slick he had $500 to spend on some hard. Slick had been looking for some young niggas to put on and had heard O was moving good in the country. So he took the $500 and told Omar, "When I page you and put 222 in your pager, come back to the fish and chip."

Omar was a little weary about giving up the $500 with no work but he thought he would take the chance, after all Slick had a Benz, so why would he do some bullshit over $500?

When the page came, Omar rushed back to the fish and chip and as he arrived, he saw Slick in the phone booth with what appeared to be a plastic grocery bag. He informed Omar that the bag contained a half a kilo of hard and that O's balance was $17,500.

Fear gripped Omar quickly along with excitement . . . Fear, because O had never seen that much crack in his life . . . and excitement because he knew he was about to get money on a whole other level.

Omar hopped onto his Honda Scooter that his dad had bought him and flew back to the country to show Tight the gold mine, not knowing the work was whip up but he got to slinging real good in a two week time frame.

He had $26,000 and was ready to re-up. Slick quickly hit him up again, this time with O's first bird. Omar was beginning to feel like he was that dude. But trouble is always lurking. With the new money, came new problems.

Omar had managed to meet a bad bitch from Puerto Rico . . . and all the niggas from the hood was in awe of the bombshell, by the name of Tatiana. Tone was so much in awe of shorty he began hating on Omar and telling shorty shit behind O's back. Omar would be out shopping with Papoose and Tatiana would mysteriously pop-up causing a scene, not wanting to lose her new cash cow. O began to feel as though this wasn't a case of bad luck, he put down a good fuck game on Tatiana one late night and during pillow talk she let the cat out of the bag and informed Omar that he didn't have no friend in his man Tone. Tone had also recently come up short with O's money, so not wanting to appear to be tripping off pussy,

Omar just cut Tone off, but being the mouthy nigga Tone was, he told the streets O cut him off over pussy and not that he was fucking up money. Because for real, Omar wasn't tripping over the pussy; because with the new money ho's was knocking O's door down. So, one night after the club Tone showed up at Omar's mom's house at 11:00 o'clock drunk and running his mouth, so O asked him to leave before his mom woke up. But the alcohol had him all ready for a fight, so Omar took out his new P89 Ruger and slapped Tone across the face, not knowing there was one in the chamber. So the gun went off and Tone was dead before he hit the ground.

Omar had officially killed his first man at the tender age of 15.

CHAPTER 2

COUNTY JAIL

After being on the run for a week

Omar was growing tired of lying in the house fucking, playing video games and smoking. He wanted to go out.

The news of Tone's death had quickly gone from front page to not even being mentioned in the newspaper. Tatiania was enjoying the quality time Omar was giving her. Lite Weight was feeling herself because she felt as though Omar was so in love with the pussy, and top piece, that he would kill a nigga over her. Although she knew in time, Omar might have to do a long bid over that shit, she was truly too young to even think about doing a bid with him.

Omar's weed habit had quickly grown once he started getting money, and today this new habit would be the reason he would no longer be on the Wanted List.

O pulled his mom's Honda Accord up on the block and all the local hustlers flocked to his side with all the stories the streets were saying about what went down with him and Tone. Most of the homeys were showing Omar big respect and looking up to the youngsta because they knew for sure his gun would bust and he truly wasn't doing no faking.

Omar quickly grew uneasy with a few looks he received from a few cats playing the block, but he relaxed a little after blowing a few blunts with a cat named Razor.

Unbeknownst to O, a crack head had already slipped off and called Wilson P.D. Crime Stoppers tip line in hopes of getting the $1,000 reward they always offered to anyone providing information leading to the arrest and conviction for a felony crime. The crack head knew he would be smoking good tonight, because he knew O was Wanted and had been looking for Omar to show up on the block all week so he could make the call.

The hustlers on the block had no idea that this smoker, who was right under their noses, was secretly telling shit to the Narcs for years on the low. What was worse, a few of the cats on the block really cared a little something for the smoker. Often times they gave him their old clothes and fed the nigga when he was hungry, and that's the thanks he showed.

O felt, in the back of his mind, that he'd been out there long enough, so he bumped knuckles with his little partners and hopped in the car to roll out. O, nice and high, pulled out the parking lot just as two unmarked Crown Vics were turning in. Omar's heart dropped when his and Officer Woodard's eyes made contact instantly.

He felt like someone had dropped a dime that he was in the area; his luck couldn't have been that fucked up! Trying to stay calm, Omar kept moving, checking the rear view trying to see what Woodard and his partner were doing. Then he noticed 2 Blue and Whites coming almost head on towards him like they were going to ram him. Omar, young and for real, was ready to get the shit over with, so he pulled over and cursed himself for having the gun he killed that fool with. It was lying right under the seat.

O sat there thinking about doing 25 to Life over this bullshit. He knew in his heart he didn't mean to kill that nigga, but who was going to believe him? Before the thought could sink in good, Omar was being dragged out of the car and slammed down while the officers were screaming shit and placing the cold steel on his wrists.

Omar's homeys watched from down the streets, knowing he was about to do years. Some felt sorry for Omar, and a couple felt happy to see him go down, because with him in jail there was no way in hell they were going to pay him for the last pack he had hit them with.

Omar sat in the holding cell with a million thoughts running through his mind. It was pretty early in the day so only a few other inmates occupied the small room: mostly a few drunks and a white guy on some domestic shit. O truly couldn't believe that his Dope Boy dreams were over, and that he stood a very strong chance of never seeing the streets again.

With the fear of live behind bars on Omar's mind, not to mention the fear of how he was going to make it; he'd heard all kinds of wild shit about being locked up. He was already seeing it firsthand.

O checked his surroundings, noticing all the graffiti with all the gangstas that had passed through before him. He heard the CO calling his name, informing him to come to the gate and stick his hands through the trap.

Omar was led to a small room to two Homicide Detectives sitting behind a desk. O's heart was beating a mile a minute. He was thinking words his father had always told him, which was, 'don't say shit when being questioned by those people because that would often times be the difference of if you walk away or do 100 years'.

His eyes became glued to the photos of Tone's dead body lying out in O's mom's front yard. Omar couldn't help but stare because the night it all went down, he really didn't stick around to get a good look at the aftermath of the P-89's handiwork. The Detectives, noticing Omar's look, came with the back to back questions with O never responding. They started laughing and talking about how much time Omar was going to do over the murder.

A part of O wanted to try to explain to the Pigs that it was truly an accident; hoping they'd let him go home. Omar's father's words kept playing over in his head. Then, he just said it, 'Man, I'll deal with this with my lawyer present.' With that being said Woodward got mad and told O, 'Yea, you all be begging to talk after a few months. Your momma can't help you now. You young cats are running around killing folks and thinking you're real tough, but there are no guns in there where you're going.' He then led Omar out to be fingerprinted and booked.

After seeing the jail nurse Omar learned he would be heading to the 3rd floor to a block that housed the city's most violent juvenile offenders.

During the walk to 3b, some of Omar's fears went away as he passed several housing units. He saw damn near every hustler and dope fiend that had been missing from the streets the past few months. They showed Omar major love by running to the gates screaming and hollering to Omar to hold his head up. Cats were calling him Killa O. Omar felt like a real hood legend with all the love he was getting on the walk to the block. Seeing so many familiar faces made most of the fear go out the window.

As Omar waited for the gates to be popped he saw dudes he hadn't seen since he'd been kicked out of high school. As they ran up to the gate happy to see him and he was happy to see that he was being housed with cats that knew how he got down.

Once inside the block, Omar found an empty cell next door to a cat who called himself Worm. O had known him from when he had lived in the city. He began giving Omar the rundown. O was tripping on how Worm was going on and on like this jail shit wasn't nothing. Omar was feeling like this was the dirtiest place he had ever seen, which in all actuality it was. Then Worm dropped the bomb on O and told him Tone's cousin was also in 3b, but he was asleep like most of the other cats was during this time of the day in County. Most got up for breakfast and went back to sleep until lunch or dinner. The youngstas in 3b stayed up all night and slept all day.

Worm told Omar that when they'd gotten word that O had downed Tone, his cousin was talking big shit about O. He was saying what he was going to do to Omar if he ever ran into him on the yard.

Unbeknownst to Worm and Omar, Bam Bam, Tone's cousin, lay in his bunk thinking he had to make his move now since Worm was out there snitching him out to O, thinking he was still asleep. They did not know all the noise the other inmates were making when Omar was being led into the housing unit had awakened him. Bam Bam slid his hand into the hole he had made into his mattress, removing the sharp ice pick-like piece of metal. He'd been sharpening it off and on for the past few months he'd been awaiting trial for attempted murder of a cat he'd heard his baby's momma had been creeping with. To frustrate him even more was the fact that while he'd been in jail waiting on the outcome, the word had gotten back to him that his baby momma was really fucking dude.

10

Now that he'd removed himself from the situation, his cousin who'd showed him the ropes on everything he knew, and someone he had looked up to all his life, had been killed by this nigga. The nigga who stood only a few feet away from his cell.

Bam eased out the bed slipping his socks off, thinking to himself that his grip would be a lot better, giving him an even bigger edge on O. He knew once he rushed Omar, he would be caught off guard with them slippery shower shoes on that every inmate was issued. Bam Bam also thought he just might even stick Worm for putting Omar up on game. But, he thought better of it because he'd seen Worm knock a few cats out with one blow. So he made a mental note to see Worm on that telling shit once they were both on the streets again. He knew how he could put the odds in his favor for big mouth Worm.

Just like that Bam rushed out of his cell straight to Omar, swinging the ice pick wildly and catching O as he jumped back, leaving a gash in Omar's stomach. He was surely going to need some medical attention.

Omar was caught completely off guard, and what was crazy was that O was just thinking how he was going to move on this nigga for making those ho ass threats. Bam Bam had truly beaten him to the punch, so Omar back-pedaled looking for anything to grab. Bam Bam kept coming at him swinging the ice pick, telling O he was going to kill him for what he'd done to Tone.

O was scared as shit, trying to time the swings so he could rush this nigga, but O wasn't as quick as he used to be. Once he started getting money, he began laying up eating too good and fucking, which caused him to put on a few pounds. Plus, these shower shoes was something totally new to him so he just kicked them off his feet.

Worm, seeing the fear in O, timed Bam Bam on his next lunge attack towards O and stuck his foot out, tripping Bam Bam.

Omar, seeing Bam Bam fall, took this as his only hope of making it out of there alive once Bam Bam hit the floor. The ice pick slid closer to O and the tide turned real quick.

Bam Bam tried to get back to his feet and rush for the ice pick. He was too late. Omar beat him to it and was stabbing Bam Bam so hard and deep the nigga's ribs were breaking with each stab. By the time Bam Bam fell to the floor in more pain than he'd ever felt in his short life, his right lung had collapsed and some mo shit.

All the commotion warranted the COs to rush to 3b to see what was going on. Once in the block, the officers knew Bam Bam had to be already dead. They stood in shock, watching as Omar stabbed him repeatedly. Snapping out of the trance an officer began screaming for O to drop the weapon while damn near emptying a bottle of mace on Omar.

After Omar was subdued, Bam Bam was airlifted on life-support to the Greenville Medical Center. Omar was rushed to the hole with Worm, not believing what had just gone down all in a few minutes.

After Omar was finally released out of the hole he was sent to court for his case. He sat in the bullpen packed with a bunch of youngstas like himself waiting on the outcome. Their future lay in the hands of the Honorable Judge William Summers. A few cats shot the shit about what compound they were hoping to hit and some hoped for probation.

Omar sat in daze thinking about his last visit with Tatiana. He could tell that she had lost faith, or was about to. It seemed as though she could hardly look him in the eyes. She told him she was alright, but she just wished he could hold her at night. Omar knew she was getting lonely fast and if she hadn't found comfort in some other hustler's arms it wouldn't be long. He knew he couldn't stress out over that because he had some serious issues to deal with. Even so, he could not stop seeing that look Tatiana had given him.

Breaking him from his train of thoughts was his court appointed lawyer standing at the bullpen with the CO opening the gate for Omar to be escorted out. He was the next black man in America to get time and head to prison this morning. Omar's attorney seemed more happy than normal.

Omar was led to a small conference room and took a seat while butterflies churned in his gut. He knew today was the day his lawyers would probably decide they would move forward with a trial. His lawyer figured he could make Tone out to be the bad guy because Omar had shot him at his mom's house.

Tone had a pretty bad criminal record and was at Omar's house, so he could be made to look like the aggressor. He hoped the lawyer was right. The lawyer had told O he only needed to convince one person out of twelve and shit could fall in Omar's favor. He figured somebody in the jury box would agree. Especially if a gangsta with Tone's record came to your house drunk, talking shit, it would be fitting for his black ass to get a bullet or two. Apparently the prosecutor in the case had been convinced by Omar's attorney.

Omar's lawyer told him that this morning can go one or two ways, "We can go in here, pick this jury and roll the dice. Or, the courts could agree to give you a cop as a juvenile, first time offender. You could be back with that pretty li' girl you showed me the picture of in five to seven years, give or take, if you keep your nose clean." His attorney told him, "Don't make up your mind too quick. Think about what you want to do because the choice is yours. At the end of the day, I'm going home, but you're the one that's got to do the time."

Omar still had to wrestle with the butterflies, but he had to admit he was feeling a little relief knowing that if he agreed to this cop-out, he wouldn't be doing Life. He would surely have a date with freedom. As soon as that thought crossed O's mind his lawyer said, "As for the attempted murder charge you picked up in the county, it seems you dodged a bullet. The prosecutor agreed to drop the charges if you take this plea today. It will save the courts the cost of two very expensive trials."

With that being said, Omar figured there was nothing else to rap about . . . he'd take the cop-out. Then he asked how long it would take for him to hit the yard. He was ready for a contact visit because the county was boring as hell.

The bus ride to Morgantown's High Rise Corrections was a long and tedious ride for Omar. Although he was glad to be out of the county, he really didn't like being chained and shackled like this. Eight hours passed with nothing to eat while a whole lot of shit was running through O's head. As he watched the city disappear, the winding roads turned into foothills and big mountains.

He had never seen this part of North Carolina and he wished he did not have to see it under these terms. The fact remained, it was what it was.

O was also getting tired of this one kid who seemed to never stop talking. He went on and on about how he had just gotten out of High Rise and was telling all kinds of war stories that Omar believed to be all lies. In O's eyes slim was not built like that. He chose to keep his thoughts to himself and continued to enjoy the scenery.

Then, over to O's right, the 16 story correctional institution appeared sitting damn near dead center of two towering mountains. There sat Omar's home for at least the next 5 years.

Once inside 3 rows of 8 feet tall barbed wire fences Omar and the rest of the new arrivals were called to the front of the bus by one of the prison's hillbilly COs who had a mouth full of that snuff shit in his mouth. He had plenty of the juice leaking out into his neatly trimmed goatee, too.

The young men were led into a waiting room.

The waiting room was located in the prison R&D Department, which is short for receiving and discharge. At this point Omar was scared as shit because he was far away from his homeboys. He didn't know what to expect as he entered the next room with all the new arrivals.

The CO had them line the walls while 4 or 5 other hillbilly-looking COs began removing the chains and handcuffs. This gave the boys a little relief after being cuffed for all those hours. Then about 5 or 6 prison orderlies came in to help speed the process of getting the new Jacks ready to hit the yard.

The CO barked, "All you strip and make a pile with your clothes at your feet."

At that time the orderlies put each new arrival's clothes in a box and wrote down each one's name on it. Omar couldn't stand the fact that he was now standing in a room butt-naked with all these niggas. The CO walked around putting crab shampoo in everybody's hair and then ordered everyone to step into the showers that lined the walls.

After the shower and a quick meal of old-ass bologna and chips, Omar found himself locked in a small room with a little window and a small desk. Tired from all the day's events he laid back, but before he knew it a loud speaker was going crazy letting them know it was morning and chow time. He had slept all night.

After dry cereal Omar walked back to his unit and noticed a few cats watching T.V., he took him a seat.

After about 20 minutes O noticed one of the new arrivals, which he knew by the name of Pie, having words with the unit's bully. Being that Pie was from Rocky Mount, a city only a few miles from Wilson, made Omar walk over to the altercation so that Pie could feel a little safer. The bully noticed Omar walk over and being that O was smaller than Pie he figured he would go ahead and scream at him, too, just to let them know he was 'the man'.

Once the bully was in Omar's face, Pie brushed the fight off on him saying, "O ain't scared, 'cause he put that murder game down! You don't want to fight him!"

Pie didn't know that Omar was more scared than he was, but O still closed his eyes and swung as hard as he could catching the dorm bully right in the eye. The bully fell quickly to one knee. When Omar opened his eyes he saw the bully on one knee, then unloaded with punches making sure the bully, and everybody else, saw that he was like that. He continued throwing wild rights and lefts until he felt himself getting slammed to the floor and cuffed by a big hillbilly CO. The CO was barking orders for all the other inmates to get to their assigned cells.

Omar found himself once again in a tiny cell with nothing but a hard bunk and plenty of solitude. After about a week in the SHU (special housing unit), he was allowed to purchase a small radio and a few snacks. He laid back listening to TEENAGE LOVE, wondering what Tatiana was up to. He knew from their last visit that she was slipping away, but he figured that being he didn't get all day, she might wait on his release. He sent her several letters during his time in the SHU but he never heard anything back. He knew then that it was over, but he held on to the hope that maybe she didn't get the letters, or something.

Once Omar was released from the SHU he learned that niggas respected his fight game. He was assigned to a job cleaning up the staff lounge. He was able to come up being that all the COs smoked and left behind cigarettes. Omar quickly had the yard on smash and quickly got into the groove and time seemed to be flying by. He started to realize he could do these few years with no problem, but he still cried like a bitch whenever his momma came to visit him. Other cats used to see him, but nobody dared to speak on it on the yard. They didn't want to start any shit with Omar knowing he was nice with his hands. Plus, his crew that he'd put together, all Wide Awake Wilson Cats, were for real on the yard. Most of them had bodies too and weren't ever going to see the streets again.

One morning Omar heard his name being called over the loud speaker ordering him to report to the lieutenant's office. He was pissed. He hoped this wasn't a piss test because he and his homeys had been blowing plenty of green the past few weeks. He knew a dirty UA would kill all hope of him getting a transfer closer to home to a spot called Polk Youth Center. It was located right in the heart of Raleigh, North Carolina on Blue Ridge Road, right across from the fairgrounds.

Due to the swelling numbers in North Carolina's prison system the Governor was forced to find some type of solution to the ongoing overcrowding. They began granting all the guys all over the system early release, parole, or termination of sentences. Omar couldn't believe his ears. Being that he only had 2 years left and was a current youth offender (CYO), with no prior convictions and a clean prison record, except for one fight, he would be leaving at 5 o'clock that very afternoon.

Omar couldn't believe his luck and couldn't wait to surprise his mom. He was a little worried because the whole time he'd been in he hadn't done shit to really prepare himself for the return to society. For real, in the back of his mind, he knew he was going back out there to pick that pack up. He figured he didn't get knocked in the past, so his dope boy dreams were back on.

Omar rushed back to his cell to pack his shit. He chain smoked for the next few hours feeling like 5 o'clock would never come.

At 4:30 he decided to let all his homeys know that he was out of there. He had gotten real close to a few cats that still had years to do and some had Life. He hated the look on their faces when he told them he was out.

Once his name was called to go to R&D Omar passed out everything he had, such as zoo zoos and wam wams to his homeys. He made his way to the front desk and the officer passed him the money that he had on his account, along with a letter from Tatiana. Omar thought, 'ain't this a bitch', because he hadn't heard shit from her in years and now, the very day of his release, he finally gets a kite from her. A part of him felt happy, but he also felt like . . . fuck her . . . but he tore the letter open just to see what was up, because he knew she didn't know he was on his way out . . . The letter said . . .

> Dear O, sorry I haven't written you in years. My mom made me feel like I'm the reason that someone else's mom is without their kid, even though I've told her many times it wasn't about me, but anyway, I just wanted to check on you and I hope you're doing well. Don't drop the soap, (smiles). I know you only got two more years to go and will be home soon, but I just wanted you to know before someone else tells you, I had a little boy by a kid named Montey. You don't know him, but he knows you . . . Shit, everybody knows you, but he's sweet and I love him. I know you understand because you were always a real dude, so that's why I keep it real by letting you know before someone else tells you, so take care and I hope to see you soon, Love

Omar put the kite back in the envelope after reading it twice. He couldn't believe it. He was light-weight fucked up about what shorty wrote to him, but said, 'fuck it'. He knew he was cool; he had 13,000 dollars and three ounces of hard white in a jacket and hoody in his closet at his mom's house.

On the bus ride home he reflected on all the cards life had already shot him at such a young age. The first girl he really ever loved had just informed him she had a seed. Plus, he'd just done years before he knew shit about life. The bus ride was all night.

Omar had met a young white girl who talked too much. She told him that her mom made her move to Pittsburgh to live with her father because of her not following her rules . . . basically her life story. But she had some good weed and had given him a few joints when she had to change buses.

Omar smoked a joint in a bathroom in the bus terminal in Durham, NC on a two hour layover. After smoking the joint, he was nervous as hell thinking someone smelled it and his black ass was going right back to jail. Fortunately for him, everything was cool and he was back on the bus making the last of his journey back to Wide Awake Wilson.

At 7am Omar walked off the bus feeling himself, with his new puffed-up body. All he needed now was a fresh haircut. He hoped like hell, after leaving the barber shop, that the little money he had and the coke were still in his coat pocket in his closet at his momma's house.

He stopped at a phone booth, called his mom and told her to pick him up from the Aamoco on the corner of Nash Street & 301; he had escaped. She was mad and told him he had to turn himself in, but he told her it was a joke. His paperwork was good. So, she scooped him up.

Omar was happy to see his momma's house. He ran to his room and learned quickly that he had his money and work to get back on his feet without having to ask nobody shit.

CHAPTER 3

GUESS WHO'S BACK

O walked around his old neighborhood amazed how so much had changed in the past few years. To O it just seemed as though so much was missing. Mrs. Parker, an older lady who lived a few doors down from O's mom, noticed O walking and couldn't believe her eyes. For one thing, she was sure her nosy ass knew O had more time. Plus, she was amazed at how much weight he had gained. She wished she was still in her prime. She would have happily given him a welcome home present. She waved to O asking, boy when you get home?

She told Omar he sure was looking good and to stay out of trouble. She thought to herself how O was a bad ass kid before he went to prison.

All older folks in Oamr's mom's housing development felt like O was a bad apple who killed somebody. They didn't want their kids to have shit to do with O. Omar made his way a little farther up the street to his man Tight's crib.

Tight was sitting on the front porch blowing a blunt with his newest shorty by the name of Renee. She lived only a short walk from White Oak, and Tight had been chasing her for a while. Tight was looking at the figure coming up the street. He felt like the unknown cat walking in his direction looked a whole lot like his man Killa O, but this dude walking his way had to be at least 30 pounds heavier than Omar. Plus, Tight knew O wasn't getting home for another 2 to 3 years. Tight knew he wasn't that high. He thought to himself, that is Omar, I knew it.

Tight ran to meet his partna, and thinking to himself, 'it's on like a mother fucka'. Omar was out and it's about to go all the way down. Tight knew with Omar home the coke prices was about to drop because Omar always made shit happen.

Omar's mom was at home busy calling up family and friends while her husband prepared the Bar-B-Que grill. He was famous for his cooking skill and seemed the drunker he got the better his Bar-B-Que tasted. Everyone showed up from O's family including a few of the family's friends.

O's cousin Tina brought one of her home girls with her who'd heard a lot of talk about Omar. She was impressed when she saw that glow most prisoners have after coming home from doing a nice little bid.

Most of the chicks who'd joined Omar's family were admiring his big arms and wide chest too. He was stretching his wife beater to the limit.

Tina's homey made up her mind that she wanted to give this nigga some pussy and fast. She wanted to be the first one to get some of that fresh out of jail thug loving. Hoping that she could possibly turn this nigga out and make him hers. She pressed Tina to make the introduction, which Tina agreed to do, but she warned her that Omar had a habit of loving them and leaving them. She didn't want to hear her mouth when O broke her heart, but Crystal, banking on that mean top piece she had, felt as though Omar hadn't had any in years. She was confident that what she had to offer damn sure had every other nigga hooked.

Omar hadn't even paid Crystal any mind. He'd been chopping it up with Tight's girl's sister, Mel, who Omar had known for years. He had always had a little crush on Mel. She was a down ass chick who'd been playing the block for as long as he could remember, so they were catching up on old times when Tina brought this cute little chick over to meet Omar.

As introductions were made, Omar noticed little momma was looking him in his eyes like she wanted to eat him up, and he was going to get his nuts out the sand. Plus, he liked little momma's petite frame and bow legs, so he truly didn't have a problem getting with her.

After promising Mel he would catch up with her and Renee before he rolled out, Omar took Crystal aside to see if what he was sensing was right. He knew his game was a little rusty because he hadn't really been talking to chicks since Tatiana had cut him off so early in his bid. Little did Omar know, he didn't have to say shit because shorty's mind was made up. The smell of O's Armani cologne had Crystal's pussy dripping in her thong and throbbing like that pussy had its own heart beat.

As the evening came to a close and people started to roll out, Omar made his move that was motivated by the few drinks in him. His talk game was coming back, so he thought. To any event, he and Crystal were on the way to the Quality Inn on 301.

Omar light-weight wanted to jack one off first before he got on shorty thinking he may bust too quick. He said fuck it, thinking about what his partna used to always say back when he was in High Rise, which was, 'nigga when we get out, we're the trophy. A bitch going to be glad to just get with a nigga fresh out knowing no other bitch can be saying that's her man.' He smiled, thinking he wished his boys back on the yard could see him now with this little bad joint on the way to the mo mo. He had just met her a few hours earlier and was already almost on top of it. He knew they would be proud of the big homey, and Omar promised himself he was going to put it all the way down for the homeys still trapped behind enemy lines.

Once inside the room, he couldn't, believe after all these years he was finally about to knock the bottom out a pussy. He hoped Crystal was pretty ready for O herself and didn't waste no time letting it be known. She knew how to treat a man and break the tension.

As soon as Omar cut the T.V. on, lay back on the bed, and kicked off his Air Max's, Crystal excused herself to the bathroom. She returned shortly with nothing on but her bra and thong. Her pussy hairs were busting all out on the side and top of her thong making Omar's manhood stand straight up in his Polo sweat pants.

Crystal stood in front of the T.V. with her hands on her hips smiling at O and noticing his manhood. She was enjoying the view that was showing through his sweat pants.

Omar's heart was beating fast as shit, but the E&J he had been drinking had him ready. He was sweating a little on his forehead smiling back at Crystal looking directly at that fat pussy print. It looked like shorty had a fist balled up in her tight little thong.

Crystal thought she might as well make the move. Sensing Omar didn't know what to do, she crawled onto the bed, removed his manhood and took him into her mouth. She was straight deep throating him in the sloppiest, wettest head he had ever had in his life. She was making his toes damn near crack like a nigga does when he's cracking his knuckles.

Omar laid back and watched Crystal work. Shorty was eating that dick up like it was the best tasting lolly pop she had ever eaten in her life. She also hummed while she ate that dick. He couldn't believe Tina was hanging with a freak like this and wondered was his cousin getting down like shorty. Omar had to admit that she was one of the loveliest girls he had ever seen. Enjoying her craft, he slid his hand down to release her bra and began to caress her perky titties.

She continued to work her magic. She looked him in the eyes like she could sense what he was thinking. She smiled and began running her tongue all over his balls.

Omar palmed her hardening nipples fighting back the explosion.

Crystal, sensing he couldn't take much more, was ready to feel his cock in her hot pussy. By now it was so wet Omar heard it gushing as she stood up to remove her panties.

He jumped up removing his sweat pants and his boxers while admiring Crystal's flawless body. He could feel she didn't have any kids because it wasn't a stretch mark in sight.

Once Crystal got back on the bed, Omar went all in maneuvering Crystal to the edge of the bed. He dove head first into her little juice box, licking and sucking and taking in the sweet smell of the long awaited pussy he dreamt of for years. He licked and sucked wagging his tongue in and out of her sloppy wet love tunnel.

Crystal couldn't believe her luck because this hunk had her squirming and groaning like crazy. He couldn't take it any longer, so he climbed on that pussy trying to stick that dick all the way up to her stomach. Omar pumped so hard and so fast Crystal begged him not to cum too soon. She wanted O to pound that pussy all night, but he was way too excited and couldn't hold back. Just like when he used to get those Butt-man and Playboy magazines back at the Rise, O shot a wad so deep into Crystal that if she wasn't on the pill, she surely would've been having twins real soon. Omar collapsed on top of her breathing hard as shit.

Crystal stuck her tongue half-way down his throat and Omar wasn't even tripping that she'd just finished eating him up. He kissed and tongued her back like they'd just gotten married. Tender dick nigga was in love.

Crystal went and got a rag and washed Omar up. For her delight and before she could get the soap off him he was hard as shit again and ready for round two. He took her out to the balcony to pound her from the back while looking at the stars. Not realizing a couple was down at the pool looking up watching O pound Crystal from the back, Crystal reached between her legs and rubbed her clit. Her body began vibrating like shit as she orgasmed twice back to back. Her tight pussy was squeezing like crazy causing him to shoot another wad deep within her tight pussy.

The couple by the pool had seen enough and were heading to their room to get it on.

Crystal and Omar woke up the next morning and went right at it again. Before showering together, Crystal ate him up again in the shower, making O promise to meet her back at the room that night.

After breakfast at the Quality Inn buffet, Crystal dropped Omar back in White Oak. He wanted to have a sit down with Tight and his other partna, Ant. One thing was for sure, Omar wanted money for real. He wasn't like a lot of cats hustling for clothes and weed bullshitting just trying to be pretty. He always told Tight I'm going to be that nigga one day and he meant every word of it.

When Slick got word that Omar was out, he stopped by O's mom's spot early the next morning and picked him up. They bent a few corners, blew a few blunts, just to catch Omar up to speed on what was going on in the streets. O was about to fulfill his dream or get 100 years trying.

CHAPTER 4

NEW MONEY

After two weeks of fucking good Omar was ready to get on his mission. Ant and Tight had pretty much gotten their own thing but hadn't blown up because they had a small problem. Ant couldn't see past a key of dope, as long as he paid his man from New York and got fronted another one. He was cool with that and unbeknownst to O, Ant had a serious nose habit that he kept on the low. Tight just loved pussy so much that every dollar he made went on clothes and pussy, so he never got past 9 ounces or more. O was about to take it there. He had informed Slick he was ready for a few of them thangs to get him all the way back in the game.

After a month or two he had come home to find out that his moms had found his new Desert Eagle and a half kilo of hard he had stashed in his room. It was an understatement to say he was pissed. He was pissed and on top of that it was his last.

His mom, being the woman she was, wanted something different for her baby boy, so she threw the gun and dope in the city dump and told him not to bring that shit in her home. Omar then realized he had to move out because he couldn't put his hands on his momma. But, if anyone else had played with his money like that, he would surely be going back to jail.

Omar decided it was time to rent him a nice one bedroom condo in the Sandy Creek section of town, and then call Slick on his cell phone to see about getting some more work because his new worker, Bubba, had just called him twice ready to re-up. Plus, his money was a little funny because he had just bought his first car, a 1990 Acura Legend, (cocaine white), with a bag phone, so he was feeling himself, but with no more work he couldn't get the rims he had ordered, or put furniture in his new pad. And, to make matters worse, Slick was in Miami with his family and wouldn't be back for a week. Omar really didn't know what to do because he hadn't really made no connections with anybody but Slick. So he was on stuck. Ant then told him his cousin had some raw fish scale that was coming back real good, so he thought, why not? He could flip it real quick before Slick got back in town. The only problem was O never cooked up no dope before, but figured he would get a crack head to do it for him.

Ant's cousin Lamont, kept some raw ass shit and heard stories about Omar and didn't mind serving him. He also had a proposition for O; he figured he could kill two birds with one stone. Omar was getting a lot of money that Lamont knew he would be getting if O was out of the way, so he told him they could open up a spot in the heart of the city and with O's rep, he could run the spot because Lamont loved the outskirts where Omar's mom lived and O had a good grip on all the money that was moving in the country.

Lamont figured with Omar running shit in the heart of the city, O would be out of the way in the country, because he was his only real threat in the country. But Omar didn't see that, he just seen quicker money because in the heart of the city you had five times more fiends and hustlers spending money, but it's ten times hotter with police and nigga trying to rob than in the country. He would have to learn that there are always strings attached.

CHAPTER 5

THE NEW SPOT

Omar pulled up on the block driving his spanking new four-runner, also cocaine white, with beige guts and too much wood grain. He noticed a vacant, run down, one bedroom flat that could use a little work, but this house was located just walking distance from the block that was already pumping real good, so he figured he could cut off most of the foot traffic that was headed to the strip with the foot traffic going in that direction. He knew the fiends that drove would soon follow. His next step was to find a good fiend to post up on the spot to help the smokers spend their money that much quicker, and also put the trap in her name. And Omar had just the fiend in mind. Her name was Rose and she used to be one of the baddest bitches in the city, but the dope was taking its toll on Rose's features. But, on a smoker's level, she was still a bad bitch. Plus, her hustle game was superior over the other fiends. She still smoked but managed to make it with her habit, ofttimes getting all the nigga's money without giving up no pussy, but also a few dope boys still on the low scooped her up on the late night for some of her sweet, tight pussy. In her thirty years of living she had managed to not have any kids, so rumor had it that she had some fire in that gap she walked with some mean bow legs, so with the deposit and first month's rent they was on.

The following night he had Rock Head Nap cook the 1 and a half keys he just received from Lamont, leaving a half a kilo soft. His and Lamont's business was growing fast since Omar's cousin, from a small town called Snowhill, was now on O's team. He was buying half a key hard, like every 2 days, that had afforded him a new truck and his condo fully furnished after the work was nice and dry.

Omar bagged up 30 ten-dollar rocks and 20 ten dollar bags of soft. He then got with Rose and made today his Grand Opening. He stood in front of his new spot and stopped all the fiends walking by his spot and asked them what was their drug of choice. If it was hard, he gave them one free and said; 'if you like this - this is where I'll be', and did the same with the powder fiends. Within a week's time he had cleared $7,000 in profits off the new trap. In a month's time he was moving 2 and a half keys of hard on the break down and one in powder.

Slick popped back up with that whip but he didn't really want it, but he kept dealing with both cats for the time being because he had built up a taste for nice things, like trips to Jamaica with his new Dominican chick from New York. He had met her on one of his shopping sprees in the city, and although she had a good head on her shoulders, she had a pretty expensive appetite herself.

Lydia was too pretty, with hair flowing down her back, she could have easily passed for Shakira's twin sister and Slick and his partner Chin noticed her beauty the second Omar and her pulled up for a little sit down to discuss a better number now that he had a few other options on prices. Throughout the confo Chin couldn't keep his eyes off Lydia. Omar, too high off the weed, he had now become addicted to blowing on a daily basis, hadn't even noticed Chin sweating his girl, even though he wouldn't of been tripping because, shit, he would have been looking, too - but, with his respect for the game, he would never cross the line.

Slick, himself, had a bad redbone straight out the hood that had often picked up money from Omar for Slick who he never disrespected even when she seemed to be trying to hold more of a confo that necessary. Omar just brushed it off because he wasn't into burning bridges and on some real shit he had appreciated everything Slick had done for him up until this point. But, as fate would have it, when Omar picked up his next pack from Slick and Chin he noticed the nigga Chin, like, turn his nose at him, and for real, the nigga had never spoken to him. But, he wasn't tripping. He just figured Chin was well connected and didn't want no dealings with a cat on O's level, and he didn't have a problem with that because he knew one day he wouldn't be doing no whole lot of rapping himself.

Half drunk and too high off the weed, Omar didn't answer his phone. Lydia rushed to get it to see if any girls were checking for her man, but it was Slick on the line so Lydia told him that O was asleep and he should try back the following day.

So, Slick took it upon his self to ask Lydia did she have a minute to talk. She thought, what did they have to talk about? But, she decided to just listen and see what was up . . . Slick, thinking that this beautiful chick had to be money hungry, said, "Don't tell O, but my man Chin, down here from Miami, was looking for a friend and he thinks you're the baddest chick in this city, and he's too rich and would love to spend some time with you and show you the world. He's on a level much bigger than O."

Little did he know Omar was hung like a horse and a pussy eating motherfucker. They ass was as good as told on. After he finished, he made Lydia promise not to tell him, and to think about what he had said. Plus, he told her O wouldn't know because they could do their thing in Miami. Once they ended the call Slick felt like he had done fucked up, because Lydia hadn't show no sign of biting, but Chin acted like he couldn't care less.

The next day, while Omar was working his spot, getting rid of the bullshit whip Slick had given him, Lydia called him to break the news. She couldn't musta up the nerve to tell him before he left to hit the block because she could tell he had respect for Slick.

Once Omar heard the news his first thought was to put a bullet in both they asses, but said 'fuck it . . . I owe the nigga 30 Gs and he can count that as his loss. He was sick of selling that bullshit anyway. So, now it was fuck Slick and Chin

CHAPTER 6

WHAT'S BEEF

Omar sat in his trap playing Double Dribble on his Nintendo with his Tech 9 laying on the table beside him and a brand new AK-47 lying on the floor, when his new 'big brick' cell phone rang, (like the one Nino had in New Jack City when he was riding in the jeep), it was Slick talking in his heavy Jamaican accent, "What up mon? It been almost two week me don't hear from you, mon. You ready for re-up?"

He was real flat with him, like, "Nope, and for real, if I see you and that other Jafakin anywhere near my block I'm gonna put so many holes in that Pathfinder that them crackers going to bury that Jeep with y'all niggas in that motherfucker!"

"What! What you talking about, mon," said Slick. And Omar finished up by saying, "Yeah nigga, my girl told me how y'all cowards get down! So fuck you, nigga! This my money. If there's a problem, then come get it nigga. Fuck you!" and hung up the phone and continued to play his game.

Slick was fucked up that Shorty had snitched, but that's what pussy do to nigga . . . make them try some dumb shit. Slick was so fucked up about it that he jumped on 95 north and didn't call him back until he was sure he was safely in Norfolk, Virginia. He tried every lie in the book, but Omar wasn't buying it and told him the beef was on site, wherever they bumped heads it was going to be automatic gunplay, straight like that.

Slick hated to take the 30g loss but he knew it was what it was. He talked shit to Chin because he now knew he would have to slip in and out of the city to hit his other workers off, plus, get with his bad ass chick Tasha, who was now 6 months pregnant with his first child.

CHAPTER 7

A NEW DAY

Omar got a call from his grandmother telling him come to the hospital because his father was badly sick. He and Lydia raced to the hospital to find his father in a comatose state. It fucked him up because he never expected to see his father in such a state.

His father was no hardened criminal, or nothing like that, but he was hard. He'd shot a few people in his younger days, but he always maintained steady jobs. Even though he never did too much for Omar after Omar's mother left, but he really loved his father. After a stroke induced by diabetes, he lay there unresponsive. Omar just knew he would never speak to his father again, unless they met in Paradise some day.

Unbeknownst to Omar, his father's side of the family were in awe of the beautiful woman with him and all the expensive jewels that hung from their necks, they also noticed the cell phone hanging from Omar's side, which was kind of a big deal in the early 90s.

Omar sat at the foot of his father's bed thinking how would life be without his father, because even though financially he hadn't done a lot for him . . . still, he did a whole lot for Omar in life in other ways. He'd always been a hideout Omar could slide to when the heat was a little hot, or if he just needed to get away when he and his moms didn't see eye to eye.

A single tear fell from Omar's eyes as he stood to leave and two days later he got the phone call he knew was coming. He prepared for the day to see his old man off, when he received another phone call that was fucked up, too. Tight called to say Lamont had got stopped on 95, in Virginia, with 5 and a half keys. So, on top of his father's death, Omar was now out of a plug and $42,000 down . . . 'cause when it rains, it pours. And he knew he couldn't break down and call Slick.

So, for the next two weeks he just laid up with Lydia with an attitude because without work his block was on stuck . . . the little shit he bought from local cats wasn't netting any real profit, so shit was crazy.

Out of the blue Omar got a call from his grandma letting him know he could come pick up a check for $40,000 from his father's insurance, like she was really looking out, when O's father had a quarter million dollar policy.

Omar quickly met her at the bank to pick up the cash and on a long shot he called his homey Mourn, from Newark, New Jersey, to see if he could plug him with a few bricks of raw powder because from time to time Mourn would slide through N.C. to buy a few guns to take sack to New York. He had always told him that was an instant come up. Plus, Mourn always had some real good powder.

When he came in town Mourn and Omar had a real tight relationship; they went back to the early 80s from when Mourn would come down to spend the summer with his cousin, Tight. They, Omar and Mourn, had become real close. Mourn had bodies on top of bodies in Jersey.

When Mourn got the call he told Omar, "Hell yes!" . . . they had plenty of work in New York, just come on up and he would drive him over to New York to holla at his Dominican homey on 149th and Amsterdam. He also told him don't come without a few guns. It would be a quick flip. Rock heads always brought guns to Omar to trade for some crack, so it was on.

Omar and Lydia jumped on 95 north and headed for brick city strapped with one Mac 11 and a few cheap Lorcin .380s to trade off for some extra work, plus every dime he had gotten from his father's insurance policy. He figured his father hadn't done too much for him so he would make sure that money worked for him in honor of his father.

Once Omar entered Newark, Mourn directed him to Hortwhorn Avenue to get a few bags of weed to smoke on the ride over to New York to meet his Dominican homey. He almost had a wreck because of the fast flow of traffic in the city.

Once they found a safe place to park he informed Lydia to stay in the car until he got back.

34

As he and Mourn walked up the block, the Dominican cat rushed up to them hollering prices, advertising their prices and flavor of work which fucked him up, but he knew he was safe, being that his Mac was tucked right inside his jacket, but he'd never seen coke sold so freely.

Once they made it to Marco's building they were rushed up three flights of stairs to a small apartment that only consisted of a couch, a table, and a big triple beam scale. Omar was amazed at how these cats got down. He could tell shit was organized for real: niggas talking to cats down the block on 2 way radios and the whole nine.

When a cop car came through the block he would hear Spanish words coming loudly through the speakers and everybody stood froze until the voice came again letting them know the coast was clear. Marco and Mourn made small talk until Mourn introduced him as being his man from North Carolina. Then, Marco asked Omar what he was trying to spend. O mar stated he had $62,000. He asked Marco could he get 4 birds of cook-up with that money and if he wanted it soft could he get three birds and 125 grams, not really knowing he could whip the soft up and get that bullshit cook-up himself. Omar took the cook-up. He knew he would come all the way up with the cook-up, not knowing that shit was just like chalk.

As he began getting his money he pulled the Mac 11 . . . Marco froze . . . thinking it was a hit, but Mourn quickly let Marco know O was down for the trade, after all, he knew he could never make it out of the building past all the workers posted up outside. Marco was glad shit was cool and even happier to know for a little extra cook-up the Mac would be his own with nine more O's of that cook-up. Omar gave Marco the Mac and the .380s.

The walk back to the car was a little nervous for Omar. It seemed as if everybody that walked the block had known what had just went down.

When he got back on 95 turnpike the ride was quiet. This was Omar's first time riding dirty. Plus, he was having second thoughts about buying the hard because, for one, he could have hid the soft easier. Plus, he had never seen the hard look so chalky. He cursed himself for not sticking to the script.

Police were everywhere it seemed to Omar, but he maintained. After dropping Mourn off he slowly crept back to NC.

CHAPTER 8

BLOW UP

Omar was back in his zone. The work was moving but not like it used to when he copped soft. Then, by chance, as he was down to his last 18 ounces he met a Mexican chick who swore out she had the best weed around. After copping a few pounds and running through the remainder of the cook-up, Omar was debating on running back to New York when Mexican chick dropped a hint that her husband had too much work. After their introduction Omar was tripping because he never really knew Mexican's sold dope. Amigo pulled up on a Ford F-150 and hopped out with a big cowboy hat and alligator boots. After a brief conversation he agreed to sell Omar just one key so O could check out his product. The brick was perfect with scorpion fish scale on it.

O's older homie told him that next time he got some raw powder he would show him how to turn 84 grams of soft into 140 hard. So he thought . . . fuck it . . . I'll see what he's talking about. Extra is always good.

After cookin-up the fish scale 84 grams at a time Omar had it down pat. He then realized that he was about to really blow.

After about two months of working with Amigo, Omar sat back looking on his kitchen table at his first ten bricks. At one time money was coming so quickly he couldn't believe it. But as always, the mo money comes mo problems. Niggas saw that he was blowing, so other spots started opening up all around Omar's spot; niggas wanted in.

One particular spot that had opened up, Rose's boyfriend kept breaking into. When the hustler was gone, Jimmy would break into their spot stealing whatever he could find from video games to a little weed and coke. After a few break-ins they got hip to who was breaking in they shit, so they confronted Jimmy.

Now it's true Jimmy was a stone cold crack-head, but back in his day, before crack hit the streets, Jimmy was known to knock niggas clean out and bust that pistol. Unbeknownst to the hustler, being that they had been moved into this area by their boss man, a kid by the name of Da. They didn't know the history on this fool they was dealing with . . . plus them New York cats seemed to think N.C. niggas are slow or something. That's why countless New Yorkers done arrived back in their city in body bags. So the young one with plenty of spunk, by the name of Shamell, spoke up first "Yeah nigga we know you've been breakin into our spot " Jimmy, feeling like these New York cats were cold pussy, plus out of line for opening up shop so close to Omar's and Rose's spot   He just barked out "Yeah, I did, pussy, and I'm going to keep on doing it every time you niggas leave," he replied, holding the butt of his nine that he had stolen the previous night.

Shamell peeped game and was like, "Alright you got that. But I'll catch you slipping and when I do you already know what it is."

Jimmy's reply was, "Do something now, nigga," feeling like the New York nigga was truly scared, now. Plus, when a crowd started to form, Jimmy's mouth got real slick like most niggas do when somebody's looking, putting on a show, not knowing one or two of Da's workers really never sold drugs. He had brought them down from Brownsville because their body count was getting too high and the police were about to lock them cats up for life. So, N.C. was just a lay-low spot for those two but they wouldn't hesitate to show Da their appreciation for bringing them down.

Jimmy walked on back to where Rose was standing, feeling himself having stood up to the New York cats. But, little did he know, that was a bad move.

After a long night of smoking Jimmy thought he had seen the last of the New York boy's leave for the night. Plus, it appeared to be dark inside their spot, so he figured, 'what the hell, I might as well hit the spot.'

Being too high, he decided to check his lucky window he'd been climbing in and out of, and to his surprise, as usual, it wasn't locked.

As he pushed off the trash can he pulled up to the window and landed right at Shamell's and Jamick's feet, almost head-first and they jumped right on top of him, not allowing him a chance to get his hand on his gun.

At that moment Jimmy knew he had fucked up. But also, he figured these boys to be pussies. So his death was the furthest thing from his mind. He figured at the most he was about to receive a good ass whooping.

Shamell and Jamick drug him to the bathroom. Jimmy thought that seemed odd. So he just talked big shit to them. They just laughed because they knew Jimmy wouldn't be breaking into the spot no more. Or nobody's for that matter.

Jamick quickly put the water on in the tub. As they slammed Jimmy's body into the water, Shamell slapped Jimmy across the face with his .45 and told him, "Nigga, you fucked with the wrong cats!" then put 2 in Jimmy's head. He was dead before he could let out a scream.

Jamick walked into the kitchen and came back with a butcher knife and stuck about 20 holes throughout Jimmy's body and watched as the tub of water turned red.

After letting him soak for a few hours they were satisfied that they had drawn out enough blood from his body, so they moved on to part 2 of their plan, which was to break the nigga's legs and arms and stuff him into a large trashcan and called Da to come help them take out the trash.

When Da arrived he smiled at the work his boys had put in and watched them load the trashcan in his truck so he could drive to the outside of the city to dump the body in a heavily wooded area.

For the next two weeks Jimmy's mother and sister kept stopping by O's spot demanding to know where Jimmy was. But, real talk, nobody knew. It got to the point that Jimmy's people no longer spoke to Omar in passing and it fucked him up because he had love for them and in grade school Omar had a light-weight crush on Jimmy's baby sister, but he couldn't trip on that. He was just getting too much money, Plus, he really didn't have a clue to Jimmy's whereabouts. Honestly, he just thought Jimmy was somewhere getting high.

One day, about two months later, Omar sat on the front porch of his spot enjoying a fat blunt, watching two crack-heads clean up his new pearl white LX450 with beige guts and plenty of wood grain, a detective car rode right up in the drive-way. He quickly threw the blunt and did a mental check of what he had in his pockets, remembering he didn't have shit but a few grand on him. He wasn't tripping. Plus, he didn't notice who these detective was, being that since meeting the Amigo he hadn't been playing the streets too tough.

The driver of the Crown Vic rolled his window down real cool like and said, "Damn, big man, that shit you smoking stinks. But, I would like to know if the lady of the house is around?"

Omar quickly hit the front door twice wanting Rose to come see what the fuck these crackers wanted so they could get the fuck out of his drive-way sweating his new truck.

Rose appeared at the door not surprised enough for Omar's liking. He peeped game and felt like the bitch knew these crackers. She said, "One minute," to the pigs and ran back inside to stash her steam and came back out and jumped in the car. They drove off headed downtown. O was fucked up about that, but he wasn't about to wait around to see what this shit was about. He would find out later.

About two hours later Rose called and told Omar they needed to talk. So he drove back thinking this bitch is wired and on some bullshit. But to his surprise this wasn't about no dope. Her first words out her mouth, when he stepped into the house was, "They think you killed Jimmy, man."

Omar said, "What the fuck. Every time somebody gets killed around here they think it's me behind it!"

Omar, still too young to understand how these people get down, didn't realize that these people don't know. They just go by your file and that's how they create their profile . . . Mo money, mo problems.

CHAPTER 9

RATS EVERYWHERE

Da drove down 95 thinking it was all good, but little did he know his girl of years was sick of him fucking all of her so-called friends. Unbeknownst to Da, she had called the hot-line with info on Da saying she was 100% sure that he had his work over at Tanisha's house, because she knew he didn't come to N.C. empty-handed. One fact being, he was on probation already in New York with a strict ass P.O. requiring him to report in every two days. But with his operation booming in N.C., he made the eight hour drive religiously, or took a flight back up top once the work was put up and his blocks were running smooth.

As he noticed a Colonial Heights, VA Sheriff's car behind him, he attempted to change lanes, not really tripping because he knew he wasn't dirty or nothing . . . Shit, all the work was safely tucked away at Tanisha's apartment. Plus, the 80 grand he had was in one of the best state-of-the-art stash boxes that New York had to offer at the time. The stash box had successfully beat the search on two prior occasions. Little did he know this wasn't about no search. They had an all points bulletin out on his '96 Nissan Pathfinder with a warrant for his arrest.

Once police in Wilson, N.C. got the call from his pissed off baby momma stating she was sure there was too much cocaine in Tanisha's apartment, the jump boys simply knocked on Tanisha's apartment door and asked for consent to search and explained to her that they already knew the work was there and how they didn't want her 'cause they knew who the dope belonged to. The ball was in her court; if she played the game fair right now. Plus, that pretty girl of hers would be in a group home if she tried to play hard ball. That's all it took. She took them right to the 5 keys of soft and kilo of hard that Da's boys hadn't picked up yet. But to Tanisha's surprise, once they got all the info she could think of, plus a few lies she added hoping this nightmare was about to be over, they still locked her ass right up, but allowed her mother to pick up her seed and promised once she was in custody her bond would be set at a reasonable amount.

Da pulled over thinking, 'damn I wasn't even speeding.' Plus, he felt as though his truck wasn't on no flashy shit; no rims, no tint, nothing. What the fuck is this shit all about? But, he still played it cool and watched his rear view mirror. His heart rate picked up a beat or two once he noticed 2 unmarked DPS cars pull up and they walked slowly to his truck with guns already drawn.

He looked to his homeboy KeKe, trying to get their story right, saying, "We just visited family in N.C. and were driving back home." Ain't nothing hard about that.

Once he and Keke were both placed in two separate cars and the truck searched, Keke was allowed to take the truck and leave. Da was shitting. For one, he didn't fuck with Keke like that, to be watching him drive off with his 80 stacks, which most of that he owed out to his connect back in Brownsville.

Once back in Wilson, N.C. he was informed that when shit hits the fan it really does stink.

No sooner than the breakfast trays were passed out he heard his full government come across the loud speaker for him to get on the gate with all his belongings, which wasn't shit - he'd only been there one night, but he knew he had to do something fast because his P.O. was already talking about sending his ass straight to Rikers to start his 15 year bid if he even dropped dirty, or missed a scheduled appointment. Being that it was already 8 o'clock there was no way in hell he would be in New York by his 2 o'clock appointment.

Once downstairs the jump boys told him, "Holla dat lawyer shit all you want to. You got 5 minutes to tell me something good 'cause I want to turn your ass over to the feds right now. So it better be damn good-I mean damn good." He almost shitted in his pants at the mention of the feds --- and all that gangsta shit went right out the window, "Man, I can give you too many murders, cold case shit."

They were like, "Yeah, well, keep talking boy," said a bushy faced cracker, with a little bit of that shit he was chewing dripping down his goatee.

Da told them how his man was down at his trap house on the run for all those murders from New York. They responded, "OK, that's a start boy. Maybe that'll help you with your situation in New York. But, that won't do shit for what you got going in N.C."

"Yea, but you know the kid that got killed from the boy Omar's spot?" (DA said thinking quickly)...Those cracker's eyes got big as a motherfucker---they just knew Omar's ass was over. "My man, did that one and two other cats I brought down from New York. Plus, I know where the body is at." At that the one with the heavy drip ran out the room to get his supervisor with his new found info.

After DA agreed to take them to the spot where his boys dumped the body, they told him he would be home real soon. If, in fact, the body was there. He promised it would be.

Once the body was safely in the morgue the round up began. Tanisha posted her $5,000 bond and was reunited with her daughter. Da's crew got picked up for the murders plus got knocked with the work at the trap because they hadn't even known he was in jail. Keke didn't let anybody know shit. He was in Atlantic City trying his hand at the crap tables and fucking call girls out the yellow pages. That 80 was beginning to get slim.

Da walked out the back door of the county jail with all type of shit running through his mind, thinking shit was a game because New York was happy with the info N.C. faxed to them, plus they were even more excited about the arrest of one of the New York 10 most wanted killers.

Omar rolled off his baby momma when he seen the breaking news on the TV: that Jimmy's body had miraculously been found and that 3 arrests had been made. O was like - damn, and those people were trying to put that shit on me. Then it all started to make sense. He had heard about the bust 5-0 made on Tanisha's apartment, so he called his man Twin-Twin, a little younger than Omar, who happened to play the streets real heavy and always knew what the latest 411 was. Omar asked him did he know what happened with Jimmy's murder and he was like, "Shit, it ain't hard to tell - Tanisha got down - she dropped that dine on Da and I just seen that nigga hopping out of a cab at his baby momma's house. So he laid his own crew down."

43

Omar was like, "Damn, that's some wild shit. I thought them New York cats went a little harder than that, but fuck them niggas, my block can flow a whole lot better with that situation out of their way."

Within a two week time span Da was back getting money and the streets was still fucking with that nigga like he wasn't a rat.

He had told niggas he posted a two million bail and had paperwork that suggested just that. And to top it all off, he opened a clothing store and a beautiful salon for his baby momma right downtown in the heart of the city and threw a getting out of jail party. The nigga entered the party cleaner than Puff (daddy) with an all platinum shiny 3-piece suit on, pimping with a chromed-out cane to match. The bitches were going crazy, talking about how fly he was and how much money the nigga had to be worth while his crew sat in jail thinking if its 30 years before we see the light Da is a dead man.

Two months later, as Da sat in the back of his store calling Keke, mad about his 80 stacks and the truck, only to get a voice mail, the feds hit the store 20 deep and took Da to Raleigh Federal Detention Center and explained to him that if he didn't come with something real fast he would be straight starting at a level 38 because that deal he made with the State ain't got nothing to do with us. And to make matters worse, his boys had come up with a plan, saying there ain't nothing worse than the double-cross, but the triple-cross, and told the feds Da had ordered the hit on Jimmy because they never heard of Wilson, N.C. or a Jimmy until DA brought them from Brownsville and the hit was a token of appreciation for getting them out of New York.

CHAPTER 10

EASY STREET

Omar drove down his block picking up his money, thinking to himself, 'damn, Da had to be getting too much money, because it seems as if his money was coming way faster now that the nigga's out of the way.' He parked at Rose's trap and told her new boyfriend to watch his new Ford Expedition for him.

Times were really good for Omar. He was enjoying the fruits of his labor. While smoking a fat blunt his cell phone rang and Twin was on the other end telling him he had just got word that Da had gotten 35 years. He wondered how the feds gave out that much time for drugs. Like so many other cats in the game, he hadn't done his homework, not even realizing what he was up against or what he would be facing when the shit hit the fan. The news had Omar thinking long and hard about going legit. So, he began looking for legit business ventures while riding looking for a new car to add to the collection.

Omar happened by a used car lot that had all types of late model Benzes, BMWs, Porsches, and Range Rovers only. So, he whipped in thinking the 740 would be a nice fit; being he already had the Lex450 and Eddie Bauer (Expedition).

His bottom chick sat in the leather seat of the 740 and his mind was already made up when a tall, older, black salesman asked Omar did the young lady want to take it for a test drive? Introducing himself as Charles Shepard, who in turn happened to be the owner of the lot. Mr Shepard eye-balled the nice gap between Lydia's legs; Shepard thinking back to when he was an up and coming hustler, back in the day. He really admired the little nigga and they hit it off, being that they had so much in common.

After the purchase was made, he told O that if he would like, he could roll with him to the auto auction coming up soon, being that Omar explained to Mr. Shepard that he might be interested in becoming a car dealer himself.

The following week, Omar joined Mr. Shepard at the auto auction. Mr. Shepard seemed happy to show him the ropes. Mr. Shepard secretly wished his son showed so much promise. Mr. Shepard's son wasn't into the hustle, being that he came up with everything money could buy. So, little Charles just didn't have that drive.

After entering the auction, it appeared to Omar that they had cars for miles; every make and model. He was amped as he heard the auctioneer announce the prices for each car, and he couldn't believe his ears. He knew that car dealers were crooks. To him they charged way too much for cars.

Omar made his first purchase: a '92 Acura Legend triple BLK, real clean joint. His next purchase was a grey Volkswagen GT1. He knew his man Mourn from Jersey loved these cars. Mourn knew how to take a certain part of the dash out where he could put a gun and about a block of raw. His next purchase was a '90 Nissan Sentra. He figured at the price he paid for it he could sell it to almost anybody.

Mr. Shepard was wondering how much money this little nigga was really getting as O made buys like he was buying clothes. Mr. Shepard, being the old school hustler he was, figured he could make come-ups off Omar, being that all the cars were purchased under his license. He explained taxes and a few other details to him and promised to show Lydia how to do all the paperwork. In time he and Mr. Shepard hung out a lot, with Mr. Shepard making money here and there off Omar, all the while showing him the ins and outs of the car game.

Lydia proved to be smarter than Omar even realized. She learned everything quick. She wanted to prove to her man that she was worthy of handling legit business and did all she could to help her man come up in the business.

After a few months of selling cars to a few of his workers and their women, Omar was renting his first spot; a location right in the heart of the city. This meant no more trap house type shit for him. If you wasn't buying a key or better then O wasn't checking for you.

CHAPTER 11

MOVING ON UP

By chance a smoker who used to frequent Omar's trap bumped into him coming out of the local gas station and informed O that he was doing some farm work for a Haitian from Hollywood, Florida, who seemed to be pretty well connected and he thought Omar should speak to the fat Haitian. So they called Pierre and after the meeting Pierre informed him that a younger Haitian by the name of Zoe would stop by with the smoker to show him what they was working with. If Omar liked what he saw then he was to call Zoe anytime he needed anything.

Little did he know his life would change forever, for unbeknownst to O, this Haitian was plugged for real. He owned two cargo ships worth over two million dollars apiece, which he used to bring hundreds of keys into United States on a monthly basis, as well as illegal immigrants who in turn paid Pierre thousands of dollars to come to the land of bread and butter.

The immigrants were also very grateful for this ride to the U.S. and felt forever in debt to Pierre and would, work for him for years just to be in the U.S.

It was safe to say that Pierre was too rich. After about a year of rolling with Pierre, Omar was getting rich, too, so he had formed a team of workers and they were all known throughout the city, so if you weren't copping from one of O's guys you really wasn't getting no real paper. Omar and Pierre had become real close - so close that Lydia often fussed that he was spending too much time with these niggas, even though she was living a life that she had never even dreamed of living and add to the fact that she was six months pregnant with Omar's seed.

After a few trips to Hollywood with Pierre, O loved Hollywood so much that it became like a second home. Plus, Pierre loved to show O off to his people in Hollywood, letting O know that Pierre really had love for him.

Three years flew by and now Omar was more than likely the richest drug and car dealer in his city. All his crew rolled around in Infinity M-30s, Acura Legends, and Benzes, of course. He rolled on the latest Lexus truck, the LX 470. It felt too good to cruise his city looking down on cats at stop lights and then pulling off leaving the wan-ta-bees in the dust.

Omar lay back one night on his newly purchased three bedroom home with Lydia in his lap, thinking, 'damn, I ain't fucked nobody but Lydia in the last three years. But, he wasn't tripping 'cause he was living his dream with a bad chick, and another seed on the way, and too much money. Shit was too good to be true. And then a knock on the door snapped him out of his thoughts. Two city narcotics officers waited for an answer (at the door), Lydia answered the door surprised to see the officers. They asked if O was in, which they already knew he was, due to the fact that they had been parked in the cut, watching Omar's house. He was shocked at the pigs popping up at his new house, being that he thought niggas didn't know where he was laying his head. All types of shit was running through Omar's head, because for one, it was only two cops and they hadn't kicked his door in or showed no signs of aggression. They asked

O if they could have a seat, which he humbly complied with. As Omar sat back in his soft leather loveseat being curious to see what they had on their mind.

Omar was unable to get his thoughts together.

Officer Bailey spoke first, playing the good guy role, telling Omar this really wasn't about him and how they knew what he was doing and that they weren't tripping off him. The local officer Bailey also informed Omar that they understood that somebody was going to get money on Wideawake, but they didn't want any out of towner to be getting it. So the only reason for the visit was because

Omar has a baseball aimed right at his head, but if he played on their side then the ball would miss his head and, that, what they really wanted - was Pierre. They've had many informants try to get next to

48

Pierre, but everybody had failed to even get close. Word on the street was that Omar was his right hand man and that he dealt with him directly. So, O. was their chance.

Omar then slowly slid out of the loveseat into the floor, fucked up about what had just come out of the detective's mouths. There wasn't no way in hell he was going to tell them shit about Pierre! Shit, he didn't have no love for these people and he knew they damn sure didn't have any for him. Whereas Pierre had changed Omar's life and he was seeing his dreams come true. There just wasn't no way he was going out like that, so O quickly said he never seen Pierre with any drugs and that all he knew was that Pierre liked to buy 4-wheel drive jeeps and small stick shift cars to send back to Haiti.

The other officer, Thompson was his name, told Omar that this shit's for real and he better think of something quick or he would be going to federal prison right along with Pierre. Thompson also told him that he'd just gotten a fax from Jacksonville, Florida, from agents on Jax station that they had caught one of Pierre's men driving a small pickup truck with 50 keys of raw powder cocaine in a secret compartment in the bed of the truck and that after the runner told them all he knew a check was run on the truck and they learned that the truck came from a small dealership called Johnson Used Cars and the runner told the agent that the young cat who ran the dealership was Pierre's main man in N.C. and it was more than likely if anybody could touch Pierre, it would be Omar.

He firmly stuck to his guns and swore on everything he'd never seen the man with no work, but if he ever did, then he would surely give them a call because he didn't want to get caught up in another nigga's bullshit. They said cool, but just know that the ball is still coming for your head real fast, letting Omar know that they didn't believe the shit that was coming out of his mouth.

As they left Omar's house Thompson said, "We'll be back."

After about fifteen minutes, Omar jumped on his CBR 900 RR to try to slip to Pierre's house to let him know everything that had been said about him and the runner that got caught in Jacksonville.

After learning of this Pierre had his people check on the runner and stop taking calls from the runner's people. The runner's wife had spoken with Pierre, telling him that her man was holding strong, that Pierre had nothing to worry about. Once Pierre's people checked with their connect on the inside they found out the runner was already talking and was out in Oklahoma at a transit center just sitting on ice until the agents could put together a case on Pierre, which wasn't going to happen if it was left up to Omar.

He changed up his whole program and started having his weight dropped off to him at 4:30 in the morning to be sure nobody was watching. He would then place half of his kilos in different areas throughout the country and different parts of the city and it worked out fine.

Omar would have Lydia drop him off at the edge if the woods at different locations and he would jump out and run in with a flashlight in his hand to find a tree that he knew he couldn't forget and bury half of his kilos in front of each tree. The following day when his workers would call, he would ride with them to different wooded areas and have them drop him off and tell them to circle the block and by the time they would come back around Omar would have the work (dug up and) ready to just toss it in their car when they came back. Then they would creep back into the city while he would just walk along the road until Lydia would be instructed where to pick him up. This move was too slick.

Lydia was the reason Omar's paper keep stacking and the cops couldn't understand why his block never ran out of work and they hadn't seen him make no moves. So they resorted to just showing their hand by pulling Pierre over trying to catch him slipping with large sums of money or anything they could get their hands on to try to make a case.

Pierre, having years of experience knew better than than to trip over one small town, so he packed up his shit and left knowing you couldn't just keep shitting in the same town forever and moved his family back to Miami.

Omar didn't like that the cops had run his connect off but respected the fact that he wasn't dumb enough to sit there until they came and picked him up. He definitely was taking notes and soaking up all the game he could from the drug overlord Pierre.

Pierre let Omar know he was a fool to sit there and wait to go to jail too, and that he should leave while he was ahead as well. But, if he chose to stay, he would have to find himself a driver to come to Miami and pick the work up himself.

Omar had no choice because he knew of nobody who could supply him with the amount of work he was used to getting and the fact that he didn't want any local cats to know what level of the game he was actually on. Plus, by picking the dope up himself that would make the price a whole lot better. But, the only catch was that Miami was 1100 miles away and that's a long ride trying to go unnoticed by the rookie agents and the veteran state troopers who traveled Interstate 95 looking hard and hoping to make the big bust.

He quickly tried his hand with his brother, who just couldn't seem to get the hustler game right. So, O thought maybe he would let him make some money by bringing work back from Miami, plus, he knew his only biological brother, and older brother at that, would never rat on him, if the shit were to ever go bad on the road.

Omar rented a nice van for his brother and caught a flight to Miami with Lydia in tow. Once he arrived in Miami, Pierre was thrilled to see his main man had balls to step up a notch and start getting the dope from Miami to N.C. himself. They enjoyed the nightlife with Pierre and his wife of 15 years, who was the sister of one of Haiti's biggest drug dealers, and the biggest that Haiti had ever laid eyes on. He had gotten killed two years earlier in a hotel execution that no one ever got to the bottom of why he was murdered. However, it hadn't been about money, because when they found the body in the hotel room there was over 2.5 million in cash and a brand new AK-47 that had never fired a round. The four enjoyed the night out, but the next day it was back to business at hand.

Kevin, O's brother had the van parked at the docks waiting for Pierre's man to bring out the load, which was 25 kilos of some raw fish scale packed and duct-taped up to fit in an open space that rested behind the van's taillights.

Omar had found that behind each taillight there was just enough empty space to put over fifteen birds. Once the dope was in place Kevin jumped on the road happy that he would show his little bro that he still was a valuable player in his organization, being that Kevin seemed to always have a black cloud over his head, and he was always prone to some bullshit happening to him.

Thirty minutes outside of West Palm Beach Kevin's black cloud showed its face when what seemed like the dumbest shit in the world happened. A fucking deer ran out and damn near tore up the whole front end of the minivan.

Omar liked to have shitted bricks when he received the phone call, but he was built for this shit. This was his dream and he was going to make it work at all costs. He had to think quickly because his brother now sat beside the road with 25 joints on him and he knew Kevin wasn't that great with answering 50 questions. Then Lydia spoke up, "Why don't you just call a towing service and get him off the side of the road before all kinds of police be offering their services?"

Thirteen hours later the tow truck company dropped the wrecked minivan loaded with the work in GeeGee's back yard. GeeGee, one of O's top soldiers paid the $2,500 tow bill and gave Kevin a ride home.

After dropping Kevin off GeeGee called O, ready to see how the new shit looked, because GeeGee's spot O.T., was dry, so he was a little pressed to get the work in the streets.

GeeGee was a real nigga that had love for Omar. After coming home from a five year bid for an armed robbery that went bad, no one wanted to fuck with GeeGee because he'd never been a hustler, just mainly a stick-up kid.

One night O was at one of his guy's spot when they heard a banging at the back door. They all rushed to see what the noise was, and it was GeeGee screaming, "Get out the house, cause the jump boys be down the street with night vision goggles watching the house!" GeeGee knew O from back in the day from when they went to junior high school together and during the five years in prison had heard all the rumors about how he had the street on smash. So, when he'd seen what he figured was a raid about to happen and go down on Omar's spot he had to warn them, not knowing that he was inside the joint.

Once they got the work and went their separate ways GeeGee stopped O and asked for a ride because his car happened to have a flat tire. Omar had a crack head meet him at the car and change the tire for GeeGee and O asked what he had been doing for himself. GeeGee explained to Omar about the time he'd just done (prison) and how he'd heard so much about him while doing the bid. He also let O know he was fucked up, which Omar could already tell by the looks of GeeGee's old ass '89 Nissan Stanza. So, feeling his old school buddy's pain, he gave GeeGee his cell number and told him to give him a call the next day and GeeGee had been real loyal ever since.

Once Omar arrived at GeeGee's house in the country which was only used to cook work at, he cooked two bricks up for GeeGee to go hit his crew off with. All the while O thought about how he hated to have to get work from Miami. O really was spoiled from all the years of having the work brought right to his door step and his brother always seemed to just not be able to get shit right.

After another run from Miami Omar decided to run to D.C. to visit his uncles and a few family members he hadn't seen in a while. Also, just to get away for the weekend.

After hitting the gogo spots they decided to stop by The Penthouse to see some pussy popping and booty shaking. The next day he jumped on 95 south heading back to N.C. Once he reached his exit he stopped for gas. Next to Omar at the pump were two beautiful Spanish mommies smoking what smelled to be some kind of haze or something real loud. So, O said, 'Damn, little momma, where's the rest at?"

They looked at O's truck and knew he had to be knee deep in the game, so they told him to follow them.

After paying and pumping his gas Omar thought what the hell. Why not? Plus, he was running real low on smoke, so he followed the chicks to a single wide trailer and he couldn't believe his eyes once they stepped out of the car. The one driving, which he later found out her name was Osilya, was so beautiful at 5'5", black hair down to her ass and a stomach too flat, with a nice little round ass, nothing like the sistas' but shorty was put together real nice.

After a little small talk, he copped a quarter pound for $1500. He told Osilya that he would check her next time he needed some smoke, and then rode out.

CHAPTER 12

'99 OSILYA

After copping loud from Osilya on a regular basis Omar learned she had an abusive boyfriend, which really didn't matter to him. It just wasn't his business. Plus, so much shit had been going on with him, a serious drought had hit and he didn't have no work for over a month. So, it was just smoking plenty of weed, hit the club and wait for something to pop.

One afternoon, Omar stopped by Osilya's spot to cop some smoke and she noticed he seemed to be stressing, which he was not tripping off no money or nothing, but when his blocks weren't running shit seemed to be fucked up. His crew was calling every day asking if he had made a move yet. Unlike him, a few of his guys didn't save up for a rainy day, and to make matters worse GeeGee had a serious gambling problem.

Osilya asked, "What's wrong, Poppi, you look down."

Omar replied, "Ain't shit, I just need to find some coke for my boys. We've been down a few months and bills don't stop coming."

She was like, "Shit, my boy friend's cousin be having that shit. Maybe I can hook you all up."

He thought it was a long shot, but figured, 'shit, he didn't have shit to lose.'

So, Osilya called O the next day, saying her boyfriend wanted him to stop by. So, he jumped on his CBR and flew over hoping they had something good for him.

Osilya's boyfriend was thinking that he could come up off O, which he could have if he didn't have that nose problem.

After a little small talk about prices, Omar said, "Just give me nine ounces to cook to see what your shit come back like." So, then, Osilya's boyfriend said give him an hour and he would return with the nine spot. After smoking a blunt or two with Osilya and small talk she really began to like his style, being that O was laid back, unlike her abusive boyfriend who stayed broke half the time.

After returning with eight ounces and an ounce of some bullshit cut, he gave O the dope which Omar gladly gave him $6,000 for, being that he hadn't seen no work in almost two months.

Omar rode his bike at top speed to GeeGee's house in the country to see what his amigo was working with while Osilya's boyfriend snorted away at the ounce he had swiped out of the nine piece.

Being that it was so dry Omar put the heavy whip game down so he really didn't know that amigo had hit him with an ounce of cut that came back to 13 ounces of hard, which GeeGee quickly went out and sold them in an hour flat for a grand apiece. After dropping O ten racks and pocketing the other three, GeeGee went to the car wash, to gamble with some old heads, while waiting for O to call with more work.

Omar went home to pick up some more money to buy a few bricks with and then quickly raced back to Osilya's. Her boyfriend had called and informed him that he could only get two bricks right then, but had O known the plug he could have gotten whatever he wanted, but her man's cousin knew the dude had a nose problem and was wanting to see who was spending all that money with the undercover junkie. But, Osilya's man would never show him O because his cut would be over with.

After the drop was made O hit off a few of his soldiers. Word spread quick that shit was popping real good and they were able to charge what they wanted because they were the only ones with it.

The next morning Omar stopped at Osilya's. When he knocked on the door, she snatched the door open with a swollen eye and tears running down her beautiful face. He couldn't understand why niggas beat bitches. After hearing all of her problems and explaining to him that the dude was frightening and fighting a growing habit, she asked O to take her to get a few drinks and she would give Omar the direct plug.

After leaving Applebee's Omar noticed that shorty had had one drink too many. So, being the player he felt he was, popped in an S&S slow jam R&B mix CD and watched out of the corner of his eyes as Osilya gyrated in the seat to the slow jams.

As O bent a few more corners he noticed Osilya slowly sliding her mini skirt up revealing the prettiest pussy he had ever seen. Also, it fucked him up to know this whole time she wasn't wearing any panties. He knew he was about to tear that hot pussy up. For he already knew that a mad bitch with a nigga beating her ass, plus drunk, was subject to do anything.

Omar couldn't believe how pretty that pussy was, with that long curly hair on it, just like the hair that flowed down her back. She watched O's eyes that were glued to her juice box and fat stretch mark free thighs and she knew he wanted her body badly. She smiled and leaned over to O for a kiss, which he met her with a little hesitation. She thought he was tripping because he knew she lived with her man, but for real he wanted to fuck, but just wasn't big on that kissing shit. Plus, he didn't know little momma like that, but looking at those fat ass thighs he gave in figuring one kiss or two couldn't hurt as he looked down at the real reward.

After a kiss or two, Omar reached down to feel that wet little box and instantly began to feel his nature rise damn near full mast in a matter of seconds.

Omar sped to the nearest gas station to grab a box of condoms because he wasn't with that raw dogging shit ever since his little cousin & auntie died from full blown AIDS. He couldn't believe how that AIDS shit ripped their bodies apart in such a short period of time and he made it his business to never fuck without a condom unless it was his main bitch, and he hadn't fucked no outside pussy in 3 or 4 years. But today that was going to change, 'cause there wasn't no way in hell he was about to let this bad bitch get away. This opportunity might not present itself ever again.

Once O came out of the store with a six pack and a box of condoms. Then he made a bee line to the nearest Holiday Inn. Osilya was all smiles when he offered her a beer and she looked in the sack and noticed the condoms. That's when the shit hit the fan, and it fucked him up to see how shorty went on some straight bullshit about 'why did you buy some condoms, like you think I got something?' Shorty got all loud and shit and started talking about, 'I got all my check-ups and shots when I entered this fucking country! You think I got something! Then, you ain't got to fuck with me! Just take me home!'

That shit fucked the whole mood up and O couldn't believe his luck, as his manhood went limp as quick as it had risen earlier for the occasion. Omar was sick. He'd had his mind set on fucking her so good that she would plug him with her cousin and cut her dumb ass boyfriend out of the equation, but now they were on their way to her crib, riding in silence.

Omar felt crazy as hell, but it was no use, she already felt like he thought she was dirty or some shit. Unbeknownst to him, her boyfriend had often made comments like Americans feel like they are better than the Spanish people who were not born in the United States, so that move was death for O.

Once at her house Omar did get some good news. Osilya told him she would have her cousin call him in a day or two so they could meet, because he wanted to deal with him without her boyfriend, anyway, because he really didn't like him beating on her and wanted to have no dealings with him anyway.

CHAPTER 13

REFLECTING ON LIFE

Omar left the hospital with his beautiful newborn which was named Nanayaa, which meant 'flow of running water' in Africa. O's witnessing child birth for the second time still amazed him greatly and also had him thinking about his future. He knew his dream of being the biggest dope boy his city ever seen was a little dangerous and could prove detrimental to his life if he didn't play his cards all the way right.

After getting Nanayaa safely home Omar sat and watched for hours at the beautiful creation God had given him and thought how bringing a child into this cold world came with such a great responsibility. He looked into her eyes and feared for her, because even though he loved her to death, the moment he laid eyes on her as she slowly slid out of her mother's womb, he knew she had strikes against her already, and the worst one was her father.

No matter what changes he made from this point on moving forward he would always be known as the guy who sold drugs and the guy who killed that kid back in the days and the one who'd been destroying lives since he was big enough to wreck havoc on his city.

Lydia sensed the change of demeanor in O and asked what was wrong. Omar, not wanting to spoil the mood just said nothing was the matter and just thanked her for thinking enough about him to want to share a seed with him, and that he just wanted the world for his baby girl. With that being said, he told Lydia he would back in a few hours and not to hesitate to call him back if she needed anything.

Lydia, thinking that since O had pretty much been at the hospital nonstop for the past few days he would want to check on his spot, but that was far from the truth. He just wanted to ride and blow a little haze and reflect on life and the direction his life was headed, not wanting to spook her at a time like this. Omar kept his thoughts to himself, but he was felling like the feds had to be onto him because he noticed that the local task force and the city cops hadn't seemed to be even fucking with him or his boys lately and he was used to getting stopped from time to time and getting his car searched, but it seemed that it had all just stopped happening out of the blue. Somehow, he seemed to think it was as though they were just letting his shit run.

He remembered times he would see police and they would break their necks to pull him over and talk shit and put the dogs all in his cars and shit.

But now, it was like he didn't even exist. All this weighed heavily on Omar's mind with the birth of his little baby girl. It got him to thinking the worst.

Omar didn't want to be one of those clown niggas to be just like, 'fuck it, I'm going to ball 'till I fall', type of nigga, cause he had seen how that jail shit had fucked off so many families where, once the backbone was gone, nigga's baby mommas would be out fucking any nigga who was getting a little money and niggas that hated you would be trying to fuck your girl just to say, 'yeah, I fucked that nigga's bitch!' And his biggest fear was his seed not getting the upbringing he knew he could provide for them.

He had also been hearing some crazy shit about niggas in the federal system, which he was totally green on; he heard about how niggas would one day have 30 years and then the next day they done beat niggas home who only had 5 years.

He'd heard rumors that dope boy Da was due a big-time time-cut which he couldn't understand none of that shit. He knew in the state joints he was in nobody even thought about telling shit. Not that moved in his circle, and Omar was thinking about this other cat from that small town called Snow Hill who'd come home who he used to fuck with back in the day. Omar had asked him how was the Feds and little did he know, but the nigga had lied to him like shit, talking about how sweet the shit was and how they had all types of programs for you and that if you took those programs you could get time off your sentence because he been given 27 years and now here he was at Omar's spot only 7 years later talking about fronting him 9 0's, which like a fool, he had done for him on a few occasions because he had real love for the nigga and had always known him to be a money getting nigga. Omar just knew it was only a matter of time before Slim was back on his feet getting too much money again like shit was a game.

After stopping by a few cat's spots Omar headed home thinking he really needed to slow down and get away, maybe do something smart with some of that money he'd saved up, like go ahead and build a nice home for his family, with a nice fenced yard and a dog out back; the whole nine yards. And do something big with his resources, unlike a lot of niggas who only buy cars and a bunch of bullshit clothes and shit never having their own land and shit to show for all the risks they took on a daily basis, year in and year out.

Once home Omar explained to Lydia that he was going to begin looking for some land for his family which she was happy to hear, thinking to herself that maybe he would now take their relationship to the next level and make her his wife, which he hadn't really even thought like that, being that in his mind, she was pretty much already his wife and she knew where those racks were at. And that alone should have accounted for something.

CHAPTER 14

MEETING THE NEW PLUG

After meeting Osilya's cousin whom Omar now knew by the name of Soto, He was glad to know he wouldn't have to fuck with that road anytime soon, trafficking drugs back in NC. He hated that part of the game. With Soto, O's work would be delivered right to his doorstep at a price he couldn't refuse.

After dealing with Soto a few months Soto really began to trust Omar and was truly happy they'd met. So was O. Soto liked him so much he started hitting him with 20 to 30 bricks at a time on credit, which Omar loved, being that he didn't have to put up no money out of pocket. He was blowing up too fast, plus, Soto's product was some of the best O had ever seen. The streets were loving it. Soto even had a mean line of green, even though it was only mid grade. He still loved the fact that Soto would send him a bale weighing 200 pounds at $300 a pound. Omar was winning all the way around the board. He would give his guys 20 to 30 pounds apiece for $700 each and then count all the profits in a week or two. With all his new income O felt no need to sit around the city staying in the police's face or keeping his name in everybody's mouth, even though niggas are going to talk regardless, as long as they think they know everybody's business.

He and Lydia and a few close friends started taking trips. One of Omar's favorite spots was South Beach and Collins Avenue in Miami. He loved the smell of the ocean and the sound of the waves at night when he laid up with his balcony doors open, smoking the best haze Miami had to offer. He also loved riding jet skis for hours during the day.

At 26 years of age Omar was living a hell of a life. Having so much success was a dream come true. Without a care in the world he was staying out of the streets, sitting on a few Ms. His car lot was doing a few numbers, which he really didn't put time and effort into making it grow, which was supposed to have been the plan to save his life, because in every hustler's mind they got to know this shit can't last forever. But, at the moment, he just didn't see the end nowhere in sight. But, no matter how sweet shit seemed, there's always more bullshit waiting around the corner, or somebody is trying to test you. Unbeknownst to him, Lydia's cousin was a real clown, for real, who was jive close to Lydia and had been playing her close the last few weeks. With that dope fiend mentality and what street smarts the fool had, he was able to peep game and noticed that Lydia had to be dropping some of O's money at one of their auntie's houses. Lydia really didn't think much of it. When she spoke on the phone to that Aunt about dropping off the counter, which she called herself speaking in codes to her aunt because she knew better than to say too much over the phone, she was really tipping off her cousin who was listening. She thought he was still in the kitchen when her auntie called requesting her to drop the money counter back off. O'd been having Lydia drop money over there so quickly lately, that she had lost count. And being the type of woman she was was, she liked to keep shit in order. For one, Omar gave her anything she needed without question and she also loved the way he treated her niece. Not to mention she was in her 60s, so she believed in doing right by those who did right by others. So she always made sure O's money was separated with the bills all facing the same way and the denominations all together, making his work that much easier. But, Ant's slick ass had heard enough, and had put two and two together and couldn't wait to get with his partna and make that move on his own family for the love of that high on the low.

He knew the nigga stayed with the sniffy nose, so he knew this nigga was snorting like crazy. But, Lydia loved this nigga like a brother and thought he did no wrong. That was a mistake about to cost Omar a little change.

Omar was too pissed! On the last day of his trip he got the call from Lydia's aunt Tina. She was hysterical, screaming over the phone, and crying that she'd been robbed at gun point and to make shit worse, she'd been baby—sitting her daughter's 6 year old son and one of her daughter's son's friends when the three men burst into her home and tied them up, ransacking the house looking for money and drugs. Which he never stored any drugs at Tina's house, out of respect.

Tina's daughter not knowing Omar kept any money at the house called the police, who now had the house closed off, dusting for prints and were trying to get statements from the kids and Tina. The nosey ass detective realized quickly what he thought the robbery was all about when he noticed right above the fireplace a big ass framed photo of none other than O, aka Omar Johnson, and when he asked about the photo Tina's guard went up, but she explained to him that it was her niece's boyfriend. But it didn't take a rocket scientist to know why he asked about the photo. The detective's next question was 'out of everybody in this nice quiet neighborhood, why do you think someone would pick your house to do a home invasion on, with people inside, in broad daylight? Because moves like that seems kind of desperate.' Looking for Tina's reaction, the detective figured they knew these nice people had been tied up and robbed and why no TVs or jewelry, or anything like that was missing. But they left it at that when Mrs. Tina's response was that she didn't have a clue why someone would come do this to her.

The detective felt it had to be a real nice amount of drugs or money being stored here by Omar in order for somebody to take a chance like that, but he didn't tell Tina anything about what he was going to do. He was going to do his best to find the people who were responsible for her home invasion. Leaving a card with her he told her if she could remember anything she might have forgotten, to call him. Meanwhile, he was too pissed, not knowing about the conversation.

Ant had overheard Omar didn't have a clue who would know to hit his spot. Because he was always careful not to be seen over there. 95% of the time he didn't even go over there. He would just send Lydia. But, he knew this had to be some inside shit and began to feel he didn't know who he could trust anymore.

The following day Tina got word to O on how much they had taken during the robbery. He wasn't tripping, he was just glad nothing had happened to the old lady over his money, even though part of him was glad they hadn't found the mother lode.

He also knew he had a soldier on his team, because, for one, she could've broken down and told them fools about the $400,000 neatly stacked inside the old floor model TV that the newer 32" TV sat on top of. And she could have lied and told him the $400,000 and the $150,000 that she had in her bedroom closet waiting for O to come and bring the little socket set he used to take the back of the old floor model and place the $150,000 in was gone; that Lydia had dropped off before they had gone on vacation. Or, she could've easily said they made off with all of Omar's money. Which never crossed her mind. Because she truly had mad love for this cat, unlike the women of today.

Omar was glad he had trusted that old ass TV with his money many times in the past. Tina's family had offered to take the old TV to the trash dump and buy her a new table to place her small TV on but she quickly refused, and they just assumed she didn't want them wasting their money on shit she could really do without, or that she was just stuck in her ways.

He was a little pissed at himself for slipping. He cursed at himself when she told him the pigs started acting suspicious once they seen the large photo of him and Lydia over the fireplace, and that they wanted to know the affiliation she had with the known drug dealer, which she didn't attempt to lie about and really didn't see any harm in telling them Lydia was her niece and that her niece's boyfriend, as far as she knew, was a good hard working car dealer who may have made some mistakes in his past, but who hadn't?

Omar took it like that and he knew he couldn't trip off that, being that the milk was already spilt. He knew when he was making moves like that with that type of money, he couldn't be leaving no traces of himself, such as a photo of himself at a spot where he had damn near a million dollars! He said to himself that it had to be some slipping shit and promised himself he would tighten up and stop being so comfortable. He then informed Tina that he would slip around her place around 11 or 12 that night when he figured no one would see him go over there. Because he wanted to look on her computer, because little did Ant know Omar had a camera on the far corner of Tina's house hooked up to her computer and all he had to do was run it back and he could get a look at what type of car the robbers had been driving in, or anything else that could lead him to find out who had tried him like that. Because, as far as he was concerned, this was just like a nigga spit in his face. He knew that whoever did this knew damn well whose money they were fucking with. He knew he was far from being a pussy and if he found out who disrespected that old lady's home and himself, they would have hell to pay. He knew these clowns had worn masks, but he figured maybe he could read one of these niggas' body language to see it an item of clothing, or anything like that, might lead him to the fools who had just committed suicide by doing this to him.

Once at Tina's Omar noticed what looked like an unmarked police car parked in the cut, but figured he was just being paranoid. Once inside he hugged Mrs. Tina and promised her he'd do everything in his power to get even with the fools who'd disrespected her home. He also told her he would remove the money from her home if she no longer felt safe holding it for him. And that he would still continue to pay the mortgage and utility bills for her, which she quickly declined, saying she was with him to the end and began to pull the screen up from the robbery.

Instantly he couldn't believe his eyes. Judging from the body language Tina and O both agreed that Ant was the one who didn't enter the home. He'd stayed out front as the watch out man, but little did he know his watch dog ass might as well went in because he was still caught red handed.

Mrs. Tina knew the fool's posture even if he had his whole head covered with two masks! She would have been able to tell his 6' 10" frame and the way he moved and ran back to the car.

Omar knew without a doubt who had done this to him. And what was even crazier, he had hit his bum ass plenty of times with too much work and he could never seem to get on his feet. But with those habits he had, who could?

He just sat there in silence for a few minutes, thinking how much this was going to hurt Lydia once O took this fool's life. Because he knew how much she loved this nigga. But, Omar knew he had to be stopped, because otherwise who knew what this clown would do next.

Looking Mrs. Tina in her eyes, O made her promise she wouldn't mention this. Tina could tell by the look in Omar's eyes that this would be Ant's last robbery. She also knew some things were better left unsaid.

To break the silence Omar asked if anybody else had seen the footage. She told him that no one had seen it. With that being said he hugged Mrs. Tina and left her sitting in her living room with a million thoughts running through her head. A part of her wanted him to smash that fool, but another part of her also felt sorry for Ant's mom, because she knew she was so young when she had Ant, and that maybe with a better upbringing he may have made something of himself. But also she felt a small sense of power thinking his ass still had no right bringing those boys to her home and kicking her door in. So, whatever happened to him, he deserved.

As he drove away the unmarked police car let him get about two miles down the road before hitting the blue lights. He knew he wasn't tripping, but wondered why they were laying on Tina's spot. For sure they weren't calling themselves watching out for Mrs. Tina.

The cop asked O to step out of the car, which he complied with, and then the second thing out of the pig's mouth was, "What were you doing leaving that lady's house at this time of night?"

Omar started to tell him to go fuck himself, but thought better of it and just responded that he'd heard the bad news just tonight and had rushed over to console her, which the detectives thought was some bullshit. They then asked for consent to search the car. Again he complied.

Turning up nothing, he was free to go on - for now. Omar sped off, saying to himself, that pig said I was free to go . . . for now?

CHAPTER 15

NEW CHICK

O shook his head as he laid back and thought how dumb Ant was. The last few days he'd been hearing about all this spending Ant was doing. He was just waiting for the right time and he would crush Ant so bad that they definitely wouldn't be able to open his casket for the funeral service. Then Omar held that thought when he heard his cell phone ringing. It was his partner, Ace. Ace hadn't known he was plotting on smashing Ant. He was just calling O because he knew Ant was light-weight connected to him, through Lydia. Ace had just gotten word that Ant had gotten caught up on 1-95 coming back from D.C. with two gallons of water, known as Love Boat, or Butt Naked, a half a key of crack, and a gun.

After ending the call Omar just shook his head and said God must be with that fool because he damn sure was safer in jail than he was running the streets. Because free, his days were damn sure limited!

Omar figured with all the bullshit going on he would start focusing a little more on his car lot. He got up, showered, got dressed, and headed out for his shop. Besides the little set-back with Mrs. Tina, his money was coming good. Soto was making sure of that. He only had to just stay low and the money would pile up. He could also be looking for some land so he could start building the home he'd dreamed of building for him and his family.

On the way to the shop he stopped to grab a newspaper so he could check the listings for a nice piece of land in the country. Once at the shop he kicked the bullshit with his salesmen for a minute, then continued back to his office.

He watched from the back office at the comings and goings of a few people stopping by and checking a few cars when he noticed a cat he'd went to school with, years ago, pull up with two bad little chicks. One really stood out to him. He got up and walked out to the front to speak to the homie he hadn't seen in years. He noticed that homie was fronting for the ho's. From him O learned that the really bad one was in the market for a new car. He didn't really say much cause he was sizing up little momma, who stood about 5'1" and couldn't weigh more than 110-115 pounds and had a gap between her legs that fucked him up. And to make matters even worse, she had on some tight fitting Spandex, exposing every curve on that pretty little body. Shorty was jive cute, too, with flawless brown skin. To O's surprise she had real hair hanging a little bit past her shoulders.

O, being a little slow on the rap game, pulled his old school mate to the side and asked him who the little momma was. Because he hadn't recalled ever seeing her around.

Fronting Ass responded like, 'it's his girl's partner', then gave Omar a quick rundown on shorty's history. He said she was 19, with a little boy.

She stayed in the projects in a small town about 30 minutes away called Goldsboro. And her baby's father didn't really fuck with her. He was married to some chick that was carrying him slick, and he had his nose wide open. So, he wasn't even looking out for shorty and his seed. That's why she was in desperate need of a good little cheap car. And, to add to the bullshit, her kid's father was getting a little money and still wasn't trying to take care of his seed.

Omar felt lil' momma's pain. Plus, that little info made him want to be a part of that mean gap shorty had. He watched her walk from car to car and was in a temporary trance. Kayla was her name. He knew he might have to bend a few rules for this mad mother! So he slipped his man his card and told him to have shorty call him if she was trying to get down with a real soldier.

He made his way back inside while his salesmen showed the lady around, even though he didn't have anything on the lot that would fit into her tax bracket at the time. But he was afraid that might change if lil' mamma played her cards right, and not just threw herself at him. He didn't want shit too easy.

Two hours later his phone was ringing with a sweet little voice on the other end. After an hour of small talk they decided to meet for dinner the following day.

Omar, who hadn't fucked around in a while, wasn't too sure if he wanted to fuck with shorty, being that she was only 19 years old and he knew some younger chicks couldn't hold their mouths shut and gossip got around quick. But O just had to have one shot at that gap. That's what attracted him the most. Plus, that walk. He just had to see if it was as good as it looked.

The next day Kayla was geared up in her best. She had begged her mom to watch her little boy so she could go out with this nigga, who she knew was at the top of his game, because the cat who this nigga had went to school with, had blown Omar up so large Big Meech would've wanted to get down with him.

Omar picked her up around six in his LX470 from her projects and every ho and stick-up kid in the building was wondering who this nigga was round their hood with that big ass truck. They knew he wasn't from the area and they all wanted a piece of the pie.

Kayla was all smiles. She knew bitches was sweating her new man, but there was no way in hell she was going to let this nigga get away. Her fucking furniture bills were due a week ago! Plus, she'd lost her job in the mall because her boss had gotten hip to her and her co-worker's scam. They were giving nigga the clothes for cost and pocketing the money. So, Omar was going to have to be her savior. At least until she could get another job.

After dinner and a little small talk Omar dropped Kayla back in the hood, which made Kayla mad because she was hoping he'd come in for a little dessert.

However, Soto had called during dinner telling him that he needed to get to the drop off spot soon, because he was about to leave for Mexico later that night. So, O being the trick he was about to become, had thrown Kayla two C notes when he dropped her off, telling her to cop her an outfit for the weekend, because he would be coming back through.

With that she was all smiles, because that $40 a week furniture bill from the rental spot would now be caught up, plus, she could pick up some groceries and get a bullshit knock-off outfit with that 2 spot. She thanked God for her stopping by O's car lot with her home girl and them, because if Omar was kicking out 2 spots and hadn't even had the pussy yet, she knew she would be straight when she put that bomb ass head game on him. She'd been taught that game by her baby daddy. Plus, that 2 spot would prevent her from going into her life savings, which was only $800 and which she had planned on putting down on a cheap car, if she ever found one.

Two weeks passed before Omar got around to sliding back to Goldsboro to see Kayla. But, she sure kept his phone battery weak 'cause she called way more than he would have liked her to call. However, he did find that kind of sexy, too. He knew she wanted to be down with him pretty bad. He told her he would have been over to see her but he had been pretty busy putting together a concert with a new rap artist who had a single out that, at the time, was climbing the charts and had NC cats going crazy whenever they heard it. So, Omar being the hustler he was, booked the artist along with two comedians of BET Comic View to come and perform. He had a few tickets for Kayla and her crew. That made her smile from ear to ear. She was also proud to brag to her home girls that her new boyfriend was about it. Secretly, a couple of her homies were jealous and had plans on putting their bids in on O the first chance they got.

Omar checked her a few times here and there, still avoiding the pussy. For one, he didn't have time to fuck with lilt momma being that his car shit was picking up and his blocks were running good and promotions on the show was taking up time. Not to mention O had a family that also needed his attention.

Lydia was beginning to wonder why he had begun to let his phone ring a lot when they were together, as if he was avoiding somebody, or didn't want to talk with her being present.

The night of the show Kayla and her home-girls got fly as they could get, knowing too many ballers would be in the place. They had hopes that if they couldn't get their hands on the infamous O, then maybe one of his boys would be down to trick off some money. They knew them niggas had to be balling if they were down with Omar.

Noticing Kayla and her crew enter the building from across the room, he made sure to slide over to them and let Kayla know to play her position, because his baby momma was working the door and didn't take a whole lot of bullshit about her man.

Kayla assured him she could respect that, thinking to herself that Lydia was pretty as hell, but thought she might be a little heavy to have a big-time baller like O. But, she also knew in her day, Lydia had been a bad bitch. But the birth of her second seed had taken a toll on her body.

That, had Lydia herself worrying, too, that maybe his eye had started to roam. But, it hadn't made any drastic changes in his day to day, and she hadn't heard of any bullshit. So she assumed shit was still on the up and up. She noticed it was a bunch of attractive women in the club tonight. Hopefully the rapper was the one who they were there for.

He watched how Kayla carried herself, thinking she was pretty mature for 19. He liked the fact she had done what he'd asked her of her by giving him his space, knowing his BM was in the house.

After the show Kayla noticed Lydia was no longer present because once he had the place packed to capacity he sent Lydia home with the money from the door and told her he was staying to collect from the bar at the end of the night and would be home soon after. Kayla slid to Omar's side and asked if she let her friends go ahead home could he give her a ride home. He agreed. He hadn't found no harm in that. Plus, the drinks he had had made him feel like playing a little bit. But, he didn't have any intention of knocking that pussy just yet. He felt as though the time wasn't right. Plus, for real, he was beat down from running around the last few days getting this whole show ready. Plus, he was about two more drinks from too fucked up to tackle that young pussy like he wanted to. He planned on leaving a good impression the first time he got off into that pretty little gap.

Once the club closed Omar and Kayla headed to the IHOP in Smithfield, N.C. right off Interstate 95 to grab a bite to eat. When O really got a chance to get a good look at Kayla, her short mini-skirt with a fly pair of stilettos. He also noticed something he hadn't noticed on their prior encounters, which was, that her arms were jive hairy, and her legs too. Which turned him on like shit! He figured that box had to be pretty, too! Unbeknownst to Omar, she kept that thang slicker than a baby's ass. She hated how fast her hairs grew, which she normally kept shaved. All in all he thought she was looking too fly, which he told her a few times, which made her night and got that pussy dripping.

After breakfast they headed to Kayla's spot. He had intentions of just dropping her off, but had to piss real bad once he reached her place. He figured he'd run in and piss real fast and get back to Lydia. She had already called once asking how long would it be before he arrived home.

Omar stepped into Kayla's bathroom noticing shorty's place, even though it was the projects, it was kept real nice. 'Kayla's a very clean chick, with a natural skill to put shit together and could dress her ass off with a bare minimum of resources and could decorate her ass off. Naturally she could make much of nothing make it look like it cost a grip and she knew where to place shit and where not to.' This impressed him a whole lot. It was a skill Lydia was seriously lacking in.

Once out of the bathroom Omar told Kayla he would check in on her the following day. She said, 'okay', and asked for a good night hug. He didn't see what it could hurt, but in his mind he didn't want no pussy. For once he didn't have no condoms and wasn't about to take that chance no matter how drunk he was. However, once Kayla wrapped her arms around him, she went for it. While he had been pissing she had slipped her thong off and now she had to go for what she knew and planted a nice wet one on O, putting her tongue damn near down his throat. When he didn't resist Kayla wrapped her legs around his waist, being that she only weighed 115 pounds. He held her up easily and his manhood had begun to stand up. Also, all he could do with her locked around him like she was, was ask which room her bed was in, and walking in that direction continued to kiss her.

Omar laid her on the bed. He noticed she didn't have any panties on and that pussy was prettier than he had imagined. Plus, it was like a little mountain! That pussy was way fatter than any pussy he'd ever seen on a woman that was so petite.

He said, "Damn, Kayla, that pussy's too fat!" She said, "Yeah, it's the biggest thing on my body!"

Omar stood her up, turning her around at the same time, with her mini-skirt up, exposing her ass cheeks. He rubbed his hand slowly up between her legs. Being that Kayla had such a wide gap. His hand found its mark easily, turning up pure wetness.

He pushed her hair to the side and began kissing the back of her neck, reaching his other hand around cupping her nice little B cup titties.

Kayla released a moan so sexy O damn near came in his pants. Kayla was damn near on fire, being that she hadn't been fucked in months. She could tell by the knot in O's pants rubbing against her ass that she was about to get a good pounding.

With her curiosity killing her she reached her hand behind her back and unbuttoned O's Cuogi Jeans. She released his manhood, trying to feel how long and thick it actually was. Kayla's heart rate was increasing by the second and her kitty cat had began to drip pussy juice. It began to run down her leg. Kayla spun around and without even using her hand, she dropped to her knees and took Omar's manhood into her warm, wet mouth. Taking it nice and slow, sucking like her mouth was equipped with a vacuum. It was so serious he felt himself shaking. He couldn't believe shorty's head game was so serious. He took all he could take before he pushed her head back.

Kayla knew she was doing her thang. She reached into her dresser drawer and grabbed a Hall's winter mint cough drop. She quickly popped it in her mouth and started back eating that dick, creating a sensation he couldn't handle. He had both hands on her head pushing her back, his knees had buckled and he almost fell.over.

Kayla, realizing he had taken all he could take, came up for air and laid back on her bed. Omar didn't even lay on the bed. He just rolled his condom

He couldn't believe on and slid into her tight little juice box.

Omar couldn't believe the grip that pussy had on his manhood. He hadn't had any pussy this tight since he was a teenager. Little did he know, he was the only the 3rd nigga to slide off into that young, top grade, pussy. And, for real, he was mild making love to her like she was the little woman at home.

Kayla was so flexible that by the time she reached her first climax she had done folded her body all the way back with her feet damn near touching her ears. He was getting all pussy and it kept getting wetter and wetter with each stroke.

Kayla continued to moan so sexily Omar couldn't stand it any longer and exploded, damn near blowing the condom off. He was now so weak he just laid on top of Kayla and dozed off to sleep.

He suddenly jumped up when the morning sun shined through the window. Realizing he'd done fucked up good and let the sun catch him out he knew he wouldn't hear the end of this shit for a minute. He looked down to see the condom was still hanging from his joint, full of seed. His pants were still around his ankles as he shuffled to the bathroom to flush the condom. He peeled off a few hundreds and told Kayla he would call her later. He hoped she caught the hint and wouldn't be blowing up his phone today, because he surely would be busy all day trying to get out of the dog house.

As Omar raced to his truck, he knew his voice mail had some wild ass messages from Lydia. He knew she was too pissed, but felt like the fussing would be worth it. For real he couldn't believe how good that pussy was. He promised himself as soon as he got out the dog house he would be back to hit that pussy the way he was supposed to hit that good, tight, motha-fucka! At the same time he was leaving the parking lot he was thinking up a good lie to lay on Lydia.

CHAPTER 16

ALL BAD

Omar stopped by his older partner's spot just to kick it with him and smoke a few blunts. Ali, his homie for some time now, was doing his thing with the green. O thought he was a real good dude, which he was, so he would spend hours just sitting with him smoking and shooting the shit. But this day, Omar had a bad feeling about Ali's new lady friend who was at least 17 or 18 years younger than Ali. He also knew shorty was always sticking around older niggas which he figured it had to be her preference.

She didn't look too great in the face but had a body most bitches would kill for. He knew she stayed in a whole lot of bullshit. Plus, he knew she had a lot of history on the streets. He remembered her from when he was on the block.

When he was a lot younger shorty was out there too, selling crack, hanging on the block all night just like the niggas.

His biggest red flag with shorty was that he knew for a fact that one of his closest friend's, who'd been killed by a snitch a few years back, brother was once fucking shorty. She just so happened to be with this brother when the feds ran into a hotel and caught the homie with 5 keys of crack, which, in return, he received the rest of his life behind those funky ass walls. Shorty didn't get a day.

Omar, not really knowing many details other than that, really couldn't say why shorty had been able to walk away from that without a scratch. But, he knew damn well that if his black ass would've been present in that hotel room on that faithful day, he would've been behind those funky ass walls as well. But maybe somehow the big homie was able to free shorty. He hadn't really heard much about how the feds knew homie was in that room or how shorty walked away. But he did know, that when you get that feeling you better damn well respect that ill feeling. He knew it was like a sixth sense. A God-given talent to warn him that something wasn't right. As soon as he laid eyes on shorty that feeling came over him to the tenth power! He tried to brush it aside, being that there was no way in hell that he was doing any type of business with her, or even around her. He figured her business with Ali had nothing to do with him. But, he felt his gut feeling was right, because as soon as their eyes met she went to the backroom and never came back out. That seemed funny, because he had known her even longer than he'd known Ali. He figured maybe she was just giving men their privacy. Omar held back on saying anything to All about it because Ali was at least 15 years older than him, so he had to respect his choice of women.

Then, out of the blue, Ali made a request he'd never made to O, which was, he needed 9 ounces of his hard. O automatically knew who that had to be for.

Once Omar asked Ali why he would fuck with something like that. He never fucked with coke and he was doing damn good with the green. This fool even had a room in his house with 100 dollar bills taped all over the whole walls; which is something he found crazy, but also funny. Ali tried to tell him that a hustler sold anything. Plus, he been seeing all those big boy cars and shit. He wanted to turn his game up. He had a nigga he was cool with whom he'd been asking him if he could help him get on with some good hard, so he'd told him he would get back with him on that.

Omar's alarms were now going off like crazy. His gut was screaming, 'this little bitch got something somehow to do with this request, since Ali had never showed no sign of wanting to fuck with hard and now he was damn near begging O to put him on with that crack shit when he was doing damn good with the green. But you already know niggas ain't never satisfied.

Right then O sat down and explained to Ali that he'd been in those streets since he was 12 years old getting money. And unlike a lot of niggas this is all he ever wanted to do and that's why he was so successful. He was in this game for his whole life, not for a bitch, or for no fucking outfit, or none of that bullshit. He was truly the real fucking thing. He then explained to Ali that most niggas called themselves getting money to do this or to do that. They had plans to do other shit, but he was already living his dreams because this was all he ever wanted to do. He was in this shit for life . . . so that's why he was balling. His point to Ali was just because this shit looks pretty, and I'm winning now because I lost for many years prior to meeting you. So, if I give you 9 0's, or 9 keys, you ain't going to have all you want to have overnight. You got to go hard for anything in life that's worth having. No faking it and no half-ass shit.

O explained to Ali that he should stick to what he has been doing, because for one, a newcomer to the shit was 95% sure to get his ass chewed up and spit out in this game. This was truly a game that had no love for a nigga's ass.

With this serious heart to heart being completed, Ali still insisted that he wanted to work. He was sure this man he would be serving was 100, that he would only be dealing with that one cat. With that being said, Omar told him being that he fucked with Ali like that, he would get the shit to him in the next day or two, then sat back and fired up a blunt of haze, still feeling like something just wasn't cool.

A few days passed before O heard from Ali. Ali growing impatient was ready to see some of that crack money. Not to mention his little shorty swore out she had too many good hustlers ready to cop from them. They just needed work. Ali being the hustler he was, figured it was as simple as the weed game -- just get the people what they wanted, then count the money, not really taking the time to understand that now he would be dealing with an entirely different, whole other kind of customer, and some who had hidden agendas.

Omar figured he'd kill two birds with one stone. Ali lived about 15 minutes from Kayla's projects. So he would go hit Ali off in the small town of Fremont, which sat between Wilson and Goldsboro. That way he could slide past Kayla's spot and maybe hit that thing again. Because he wasn't really satisfied with his performance on their first go around. Not to mention that tight little juice box had been on his mind constantly since their first sexual encounter.

After hitting Ali off Omar sped to Kayla's house, who was also ready to show Mr. O what she was really made of. She could sense by their last few phone conversations that he was lightweight feeling her. So, she knew their next encounter she would have to pour it on heavy.

That way, maybe he would begin to spend some quality time with her. And maybe even play daddy to her fatherless child because her kid's father's nose was so far up his wife's ass that he wasn't even claiming his son with Kayla.

He knocked on Kayla's door. She answered quickly, ready to show off her see-through nightgown that she'd put on as soon as he called letting her know he was on his way over. Once Omar saw what she was wearing he instantly began to get an erection. She was looking so amazing. Not to mention, the cheap gown was see-through, riding real high on her thighs. Seeing what it was, he wasted no time dropping his pants to his ankles right in the living room . . . and Kayla, figuring now or never, seen his manhood hard and pointing towards the clouds, dropped right to her knees. Never even touching it with her hands, she took him right in her mouth. Putting in some work, she made it a whole lot better than he received at home. She was making his knees buckle from time to time. She was truly good at her craft, and O, not wanting to bust too quickly had to push her head back, because she was going like her life depended on it. Which, in a sense, it did. Once he pushed her back she knew she was working her magic right and went right back on that dick like it was the best tasting lollipop she'd ever had.

He literally had to force her off that dick, then laid her across the couch, noticing she didn't have on any panties. He also noticed her once shaved pussy was now covered in hair, which he also loved. He knew she had let it grow out because he'd told her how that had always turned him on.

Once inside that tight box he had to cover her mouth with his hand because she was moaning so good there was no way in hell he was going to be able to hold that first nut much longer. As he pumped away he noticed she was trying to tell him something so he removed his hand to hear Kayla saying, "baby when you get ready to cum . . . put it in my face." And that did it.

Omar couldn't hold it no longer. Snatching it out he raised his manhood up to her mouth. She jumped on it, going crazy once again, not allowing a single drop to touch the floor. She continued to suck and pull until he was erect again; which was something else O had never experienced with Lydia.

O was now in heaven!

Kayla seeing that he was ready for round two, turned around and got on all fours. He took her from the back, pumping in and out. Kayla was loving this, thinking to herself, she'd done a good job and he would either fuck with her hard, or fall back. Either way she knew she'd put her best foot forward and just hoped he would go with the latter. Before she knew it that tight box had him collapsing on her back, damn near out of breath, too happy with today's meeting, knowing in his mind he would truly be back for this young thing again.

After taking Kayla to the steak house for a nice meal and stopping by her mom's spot to meet Kayla's mom and her little son, Omar headed back to Wilson.

He got a call from Ali saying that shit was going well and he would need to see him again in the next day or two, which he thought was odd, being that this was Ali's first pack, but not really giving it too much thought. Omar's mind was back on that mean piece of work that had just gotten put on him.

CHAPTER 17

SLIPPING

Omar was truly feeling himself lately and Lydia could lightweight tell something was up, but couldn't put her finger on it. She figured she was tripping because whatever was going on with him, it couldn't be no bullshit with their relationship, because he was moving forward with their plans on building a home for their growing family. Today they'd just paid for 2 acres of land in the country and had made arrangements with a contractor to begin building a 3500 square foot home. So whatever was up with O, it seemed as though his family was his number one priority.

Little did Lydia know Omar's nose was tore wide open over that young thing he had in Goldsboro. He'd done gave her a nice Honda Accord so she could meet him at any time he desired her skillful mouth game and tight little box.

He had even gained so much trust in Kayla he had begun hiding bricks and pounds in her home. And if he needed a quick brick dropped here or there, he would just call her and have her grab one to meet one of his little partners wherever and drop that. So now she was keeping 2 to 3 thousand dollars in her pockets, stunting on her little home girls who were now too sick. She was the one to catch the big fish.

Little did Omar understand or realize the law of the universe is if you do people wrong, you would more than likely run into some bad luck.

While Lydia sat home doing all the right things by Omar; like running to the contractor office handling the home building process and taking care of the affairs at the car lot, making sure his money was steady growing, he would be laying up with young thing. Lydia had by now realized, too, that he was fucking around. He'd began to slip like the night he dropped Kayla off the Honda on her birthday. Then had Kayla drop him off at home around 3 in the morning, thinking Lydia would be fast asleep. But she wasn't. She'd been up with the baby and had noticed the lights turn into the driveway. Since she was up she headed to the door to open it for Omar. Omar, slipping, had sat in the car a few minutes, still talking to Kayla.

Omar got out of the car not realizing Lydia was standing at the front door and she noticed the young woman in the driver's seat who was all smiles when the interior light came on when he was getting out of the car. Seeing the pretty young girl broke Lydia's heart because at that time of morning what in the fuck was her man doing with some bitch. And to make shit more obvious

He tried to lie, not knowing she'd seen Kayla when the dome light came on.

He tried telling Lydia it was one of his homies dropping him off. So Lydia really knew now her hunch was right. This had Omar in the dog house for a few weeks. To make shit worse, Lydia being the chick she was, went on a full investigation. She'd gotten his cell phone bill and traced Kayla's number down simply by calling the numbers he had been calling on those late nights.

Omar came in all late one night about a month after that first incident. He slipped again, calling himself going to Kayla for a quickie. After they fucked a couple of rounds, he didn't shower, he just washed his manhood and went home.

Lydia, now to the point of stressing all the way out, would be waiting up when Omar came in, wanting sex just to see if he even wanted some pussy. Or if the nigga could even get it up, which wasn't a problem with him. He loved being out fucking then coming home for a quick one, but this night being that he didn't shower he smelled just like Kayla's expensive perfume and didn't even realize it.

After that last blunt and work out Kayla put on him he wasn't thinking about nothing but going to bed. So when Lydia forced the pussy on him he figured a quick one in her then he could get some sleep without all the fussing she'd been doing lately.

Once up in the pussy, he noticed tears running down Lydia's cheeks. He stopped hitting the pussy, like, what the fuck's wrong with you, when her reply was I can smell that bitch all over you nigga, then jumped out the bed screaming, I'm going to kill you, nigga, fucking that bitch then coming home fucking me, she screamed, waking the kids up and all.

He was too mad but in the back of his mind he knew this was all his fault. But that young pussy had him tripping. For the next two weeks Omar stayed in, not really going out much without Lydia with him. Even that didn't stop Lydia from calling Kayla's phone. But Kayla refused to speak to her and just changed her number every time.

Lydia would catch him slipping and pick up on what numbers was suspect on his phone bill until he had to stop his billing from coming to his address altogether.

Omar was thinking something's got to give. All this headache Lydia was giving him. He wasn't sure he was ready to do the family thing anymore. But, he loved his kids so much he couldn't see not staying with them even if he wasn't sure if Lydia was the one for him anymore. Breaking him from his thoughts he got a call from some nigga he didn't know, but once the caller confirmed that it was Omar he was speaking to, he hit him with the bad news that Ali had just gotten popped with the 9 ounces of hard that he had hit him with the day before and needed Omar to have a bail bondsman come to get him.

Omar made it his business to never deal with nobody after they got hit and knew his and Ali's friendship was now over and he needed to think how to handle this situation. First, he drove about 30 minutes away to Raliegh. He'd cop'd him a small one bedroom apartment in a section of Raleigh that was about 15 minutes away from any hood on the north side. It was a few blocks from Tower Shopping Center, an ideal spot for him to slip away with some work, cook it on the low, and slide it back to the Wilson area without anyone having a clue where he would be. Omar would also slide Kayla through from time to time to blow her back out. She'd move the work around for him, so he was never dirty for real.

After calling his main bondsman he laid back waiting to hear what had happened. Knowing in his mind that giving Ali that shit in the first place was a bad idea. But niggas always on some monkey see monkey do shit.

Ali just had to go outside his element. Now he want a nigga to get him out of jail. He knew never to go against his gut and at the same time he didn't realize he put that bad karma on himself not being 100 with his woman who'd been 100 with him from the door.

After waiting an hour and a half his bail bondsman called back and told him that Ali had already made bond by the time he'd gotten up there, so that put him on edge as well, because if the nigga was out why hadn't he called Omar and let him know what was going on. He wanted to know if his name had somehow came up in this shit and what had happened in the first place.

He was blowing blunt after blunt trying to play some Madden couldn't really get into the game. He was ready to know what had went down with Ali. Breaking him away from his thoughts, his cell began to ring with Ali's number showing up on the caller ID. Now, all of a sudden, Omar didn't really want to talk to this fool, but answered. Ali went straight to the point. Ali asked him to meet him at Pender Street Park, which he agreed to do.

Forty-five minutes later Omar parked his Dodge Neon, the car he drove when he wanted to be on the low, and walked over to Ali and shook his hand and hugged him, trying to feel the nigga's chest a little, trying to see if the nigga was wired or some shit. Faking like he was really concerned, he asked Ali was he OK, and did he have money for a lawyer, next asking him what the fuck happened.

Ali went on to tell Omar he knew who had got him fucked up. Some nigga O had never heard of, from a block called Snowden Dr., who drove a white Honda.

Omar told him he'd never heard of that homie. So Ali went on to say the first few times he served Slim, it was all good. He stopped him and asked, 'where did you find this nigga', and just like he figured, the lit bitch Ali was fucking made the introduction. Then, what really blew Omar was Ali told him the nigga had been buying O's from him at $900 a piece.

Omar said, "I would've told you that was the police'. Ain't nobody in this city paying that shit. I got the city on smash, and the most nigga's getting is 750-tops. Because all my crew hitting for the $600. So, I could've told you your man had to be the police.

Next he wanted to know, 'how they knock you with your whole pack, then just shook his head when he learned this fool had all his eggs in one basket.

Ali told him the nigga had called him and asked for him to meet at their spot they'd been meeting at and gave him the code for 2 slips. So, Ali said as usual he made the short drive to the location. Once there he noticed a cop car on the corner that could've pulled off, but had waited for Ali to pass by, then pulled right out behind him. He knew right then what it was once 5.0 hit him with the flasher. He found a spot, pulled over and tried his hand on foot. After a brief foot chase the well trained cop had Ali run down. Then quickly found the 2 slips Ali threw in the bushes, along with the 9mm under the seat of his car. By that time the task force were on the scene. They then informed Ali they were headed back to Ali's house to search. That's where they found the other 7 ounces of crack.

Then he asked how he had gotten out so quick, because he'd sent a bail bondsman downtown to get him and he'd already been released.

Ali, to Omar's surprise didn't play any games. He told O, 'look man, the only reason I'm out is for you. I had to tell them I would set you up, or they said they were going to hold me without bail and that if I didn't make that happen, I would be facing 10 years to life.'

Omar thought that was bullshit. It was 2001. He didn't even know 9 slips would fuck you off like that. For one, to him, 9 slips wasn't shit. He played with bricks of crack near on a daily basis.

He said to Ali, 'man them people lying like shit. How the fuck you facing time like that? You ain't even on probation or nothing and you've never even been busted.'

Ali said he wasn't sure, but once he got a lawyer, he would let him know.

He gave his word on his life that he would never set him up. He just agreed to do so to get out because they show'd him photos of him and

Omar sitting on his porch on different days smoking and kicking it. So, they said they knew I knew you and that they knew that was Omar's shit he'd been caught with. He kept reassuring him that he would never do no shit like that and that's why he was telling O everything they said. He just wanted a few weeks to get his shit in order in case he would have to lay it down for the next 10 to 20 years. He also told him, 'man I could never do you that way, man. You begged me not to fuck with that shit. All I had to do was stick to my thing, but that bitch swore everything was good with dude.'

He had heard enough and was about to roll when Ali said something that really fucked him up. He told Omar, 'man they know about the home you building and everything.' That fucked O up because he'd just started that project way out in the country. He thought who the fuck told them that. Ali also told Omar something that made him feel like he'd been moving real slick. Ali was like, "I was listening to them. They want you bad. But I can tell you they don't got nothing on you. All you got to do right now is just quit. You got everything a nigga could want. If you quit now, you got they ass. You can walk away clean.'

Hearing that Omar was feeling himself, and told Ali, 'fuck them people! They can't see me. Next time you talk to them, tell them I said what they waiting for?', and O walked away, telling Ali, 'call me when you find a lawyer'.

O still not fully believing all that Ali said felt as though the old head was being real with some of what he said. He would just play him from a distance to see how shit looked in the next few weeks.

Two months passed without a word from Ali. Omar pretty much wasn't even thinking about him no more or the feds, he just was sure to move extra careful and swore there was no way in hell he was letting any new faces in his world. Then one day he, Lydia, and the kids were going grocery shopping when he noticed a cat fitting Ali's description painting on the burger joint next to the grocery store calling out his name.

He was feeling a little fucked up because the man seemed to be playing fair and he hadn't even checked on the nigga to see if he needed $5.00 for a fucking sandwich or anything, but niggas wasn't too crazy about fucking with no nigga who talking that fed shit. Once over there, O, holding back a laugh, looking at how dirty Ali was being, that he'd never seen him looking like that, asked how he'd been. Ali was like, he was being cool, just trying to save all the money he could for when he had to go in. He then told Omar that those people weren't faking with him and that he had to sign a plea for 10 to life about a week ago, which he still found hard to believe, for that little bit of shit, but Ali swore to him that's how it was going down. Ali also told him they were upset when he told them that O refused to deal with him anymore, but his court appointed lawyer had convinced them to let him stay out on "house arrest" so he could work, and maybe get Omar to change his mind before Ali's sentencing date came up, which Ali and O knew that would never happen.

Omar still not 100% sure about Ali told him he'd took his advice and had chilled all the way out. As he walked away Ali said, "Yeah, homie, do it for your kids player. They're going to need their father."

That was the last time he saw Ali. About three months later Ali's uncle stopped by his car lot with Ali's contact info and told him Ali had gotten 188 months in federal prison and that he was at F.C.I. Butner. After hearing this Omar was at a loss for words and couldn't understand how they gave that kid damn near 16 years for that little shit. He wondered if he ever got snatched what would his sentence be. Which, for real, he couldn't see him slipping like that. He also figured his paper was way too long for him to even get 2 or 3 years. He would just pay his way out of that shit if it ever came down to it.

Omar not knowing these people were knocking niggas's heads off with that 100 to 1 ratio shit. Little did he know it was niggas in the feds that weren't even getting no money for real, who were just getting high and because of their prior criminal history and that ratio had 30 and better for a lot less than 9 zips and a pistol. Little did he know, ignorance of the law damn sure wasn't going to help him; or the next motherfucker who stood in front of that judge with that crack case.

CHAPTER 18

WATCH YOURSELF

Omar truly felt bad for Ali and had every intention of looking out for him throughout his incarceration, even though he had begged the nigga to stay in his lane. But, as the weeks turned into months, and the years flew by, Omar had pretty much forgot all about him. His focus was back on doing him; finishing up his new home and buying all the finest furniture to complement his new dream house. He was really living his dope boy dreams. He had the illest house and his car game was up. He'd just copped the S500 Benzo to park in his double garage. Had two bad bitches, and had just been introduced to a bad Puerto Rican mama named Sasha who gave J-Lo a run for her money.

Sasha was too bad. She just moved to N.C. with her cousin, from N.Y., to surround themselves with other family that had migrated to the Carolinas years earlier trying to get away from the fast pace of the city. Not to mention Sasha's man had just gotten 27 years in the Feds for C.C.E.

Sasha was use to niggas that were getting money. She was introduced to Omar by her cousin who had blown O's name up so crazy to her he really didn't have to say much because her mind was pretty much made up that this was going to be her new meal ticket. She had no regards to the fact that this man already had a woman at home with two kids. She was trying to make sure Sasha was cool. Not to mention the fact that she heard all about the big ass home he'd just built. Her mission was now to get up in there by any means. Once they were introduced Omar was impressed with little mamma. She was by far one of the baddest bitches in his city if not the baddest, and like every other nigga in the city he wanted to see if that pussy was as good as it looked. Sasha also had business about herself. She kept a good job and had transferred from the First Union out in New Jersey to the bank in Wilson.

Omar liked the fact that she had a career, unlike his two present chicks who pretty much lived completely off him, which he wasn't tripping and had preferred for Lydia to be a stay at home mom.

Once he got a taste of what Sasha had to offer it was pretty much downhill for his relationship with Lydia and Kayla. Not only was Sasha's pussy game through the roof, her head game was damn near as good as Kayla's. Within a six month time frame Omar was pretty much living with Sasha in a nice 4 bedroom home he'd put twenty grand down on, not to mention the eleven grand he kicked out on her credit card bills making her credit score good enough to purchase the $250,000 home.

Sasha knew she'd hit the jackpot with O. She'd had a few ballers in her day but none that kicked out the paper like Omar.

Niggas in New Jersey had spent money fucking with her but in New York there was bad bitches like Sasha everywhere, so her stock wasn't as high in New York like it was in NC. Sasha was living so good she'd even moved her mom in with her.

Lydia, hearing all the rumors, cried herself to sleep many nights over the blatant disrespect Omar was showing. He even felt bad about it himself, but Sasha's pussy was so bomb he couldn't stay in it 5 minutes without coming all over himself.

Kayla also was feeling the effects of this new relationship. Omar barely giving her the time of day, unless he needed her to make a move for him. She was trying everything to win some quality time from him. She'd also convinced him to start hitting her cousin Coco off with one half bricks, trying to show Omar she was worth more than just the sex, which, for real, she was. She truly loved the ground this nigga walked on and told him on several occasions she didn't mind being the side chick as long as he spent some time with her.

But shit would soon go all bad. One night after Coco had picked up a half of bird from Kayla, he got pulled and knocked with the work and quickly began telling everything he knew after a few days in county. The fed's told him they'd been on Omar's trail for a while now and that if he could make something happen with Omar this situation would be looking a whole lot better, which he swore out he could.

Back on the street Coco tried to get Kayla to call Omar for more work, which she saw no need in that when she already had it. But she really didn't think nothing of it when he keep wanting to speak with him directly. He quickly blamed it on him wanting to see if he would give him a better number. The only problem was, Kayla couldn't get in touch with O her damn self. Half the time Sasha had Omar almost to the point to where he wouldn't even talk to his baby mama in front of Sasha.

Omar had truly fell weak for Sasha in less than a year's time. He pretty much wanted to marry her, which really wasn't a good idea. Little did he know that from time to time when Sasha would go back to New York with her cousins they still had niggas they were fucking around with.

CHAPTER 19

SIGN OF THE TIMES

Soto called Omar to introduce him to his brother Fernando, who would now be stepping in to take Soto's spot. Soto now pretty much rich enough to return home to Mexico City with his young wife had plans on opening a gas station and starting his own rodeo back home. He was pretty much set. O wasn't tripping on who gave him the shit as long as it kept coming. Soto also wanted him to take a trip with him to show him what all the hard work had afforded him because unbeknownst to O, Soto really liked him and had noticed Omar's hustle wasn't like it was when they first met.

On their trip to Mexico he asked Omar straight up what was up with him.

Omar told him about Sasha, explaining to him how good the sex was and how much he was feeling her. Soto thought this was some weak shit and if he hadn't really grown to really have love for this young nigga he would've pulled back from him, but he hoped the youngster would wizen up. He also told Omar that beautiful women were everywhere and that he should never let some random chick come between what took so many years to build. Plus, Soto had met Lydia many times and thought she was a beautiful woman, too. Also very faithful.

Omar felt him and understood perfectly where he was coming from, but in his mind he wasn't planning on cutting Sasha loose any time soon, unless she did some real bullshit.

Once in Mexico, Omar couldn't believe how fucked up people were living outside of the resort towns. This, too, helped him understand why the Amigos go so hard to get their money and why so many are crossing the border trying to get that American dream.

Soto really knew Omar was fucked up over Sasha when he tried to turn O on to a couple Spanish mamas that were too beautiful and Omar seemed to only want to smoke weed and talk on the phone with Sasha.

Omar had admired the nice home Soto had with many acres of land. Soto raised cattle and chickens. Soto also had a barn behind his home that was pretty much full of weed and bricks of the best cocaine money could buy, ready to be packed and shipped into the United States.

The night before Omar was set to leave, Soto figured he'd show O that he had love for him and wouldn't hesitate to kill for him and his movement.

About two months prior to their trip there was a runner who had delivered 30 keys to Omar that were all fucked up. When O opened one to cook only about half the work would come back. It was cut to death and didn't even have Soto's stamp in the middle of the bricks. Omar had called Soto several times telling him to come back and get the work. O didn't know but the runner had also dropped off a few hundred bricks in ATL that were mostly fucked up. Omar knew something wasn't right as soon as he opened one. Usually the work would look like you could see diamonds in it, plus normally a stamp of horses running would be on the bricks, or maybe dolphins jumping, or a scorpion. But the work damn near looked like chalk.

Soto was so mad he told O he could have the shit. Soto who was really an easy-going laid back guy asked Omar to come for a ride on some four wheelers with him, which he had complied.

About two miles into a wooded area they came to what appeared to be an old abandoned warehouse. Once inside Omar noticed the cat who dropped the 30 keys of bullshit tied up laying in the corner bleeding like shit, plus a heavy set woman also lay in a puddle of blood who began screaming something in Spanish. Also in the warehouse were 2 younger looking Mexicans who both had AK-47s, standing near the runner and a woman. Soto walked to the runner and asked him did he feel as though stealing from him was worth the risk. All the runner did was ignore the question and continued to beg for his and the woman's lives, who Omar now knew was the runner's sister. O hoped to get the fuck away from there. He definitely wasn't trying to get locked up way out that motherfucker. Plus, he had noticed that his piss had been mighty hot the last two days. He hoped like hell he wasn't burning from a STD, because who could he blame for fucking him up when he was fucking 3 bitches? No sooner than that thought crossed his mind, Soto put 2 in the woman's head, as her brother screamed for mercy. Soto silenced his cries as well with 2 to the back of his head, then told Omar 'let's ride.'

Omar was fucked up about that and also wondered why did Soto feel the need to show O he'd done that to those people because of the inconveniences they'd caused Omar and himself. Soto wanted O to know too, that shit wasn't at all a game with him, being that he was noticing Omar beginning to show weakness.

Soto knew from experience that pussy was the number one killa in the world. A lot of niggas were dead or in jail behind pussy, one way of the other.

A lot of niggas had turned rat trying to get back home to some ho-ass bitch.

The next morning they crossed back over to the United States. Omar had a lot on his mind having just witnessed a double murder. Not to mention, he was now sure his dick was on fire, sticking to his boxers and some mo shit.

Once back in Wideawake Wilson, O didn't know what to do but just go ahead to the health clinic and get his shit together.

Omar almost screamed when the white woman stuck a long piece of metal inside his joint. It wasn't even so much the pain it was just witnessing that metal going inside the tip of his penis. After the woman ran a few tests she came back with the news. O pretty much already knew he had contracted an STD called gonorrhea. He was too embarrassed but was glad to know within a few days all symptoms would be gone. The nurse also spoke to Omar about the importance of practicing safe sex and gave him a whole rack of condoms.

Omar left the clinic wondering which one of those bitches were fucking on him. He knew that they all have to have the STD because before leaving town he'd pretty much slept with all 3 women back to back.

In his heart, even though it hurt like shit, Omar felt very strongly that Sasha was the guilty party. For one, he'd been fucking Kayla and Lydia for years now, and nothing like this had ever come up. He knew Sasha loved to run back to the city every chance she got. Omar also had the dilemma of telling all 3 women that they needed to go to the clinic because he sure as hell wasn't fucking any of them until they got they shit together. He knew telling Lydia was going to be the hardest because, shit, they lived together. Plus, she'd been accusing him of cheating for a minute now. Also in a fit of rage, after they had a huge argument, screamed to him he was going to catch AIDS fucking those ho's in the street.

Omar decided to tell Sasha first because, for real, it hurt him the most, because he felt she was the one.

Sasha took the news a little easier than he assumed, but quickly put a spin on it talking about, 'Yeah nigga, Mrs. Lydia ain't as slow as you think. While you out with me she probably called herself getting your ass back.'

Omar wanted to slap the shit out of her. He would've bet his last dollar Lydia hadn't did no shit like that. Sasha being the most experienced out the bunch with relationships knew exactly how to play he and could tell he'd caught an attitude. She acted like she wasn't even mad and called the clinic to make an appointment for the following day, and told Omar she would never do him like that. And as a matter of fact, as long as he stayed with Lydia he would have to use a condom when he was fucking her. That way, when he got burnt again he would automatically know it wasn't her.

Sasha was quick on her feet and even went so far as to tell Omar the next day that she went and got tested and didn't have shit so he couldn't of got it from her . . . lying like shit. She knew the last time her and her cousin had went to New York they'd went out partying. She had a few drinks too many and woke up the next morning butt naked in bed with a smooth talking nigga she'd met at the bar, whom she hadn't even spoke to since, because she felt so stupid for doing it even though she swore to her cousin, who'd did the same shit on the previous occasion herself in the past, that if she wanted to have sex on the first night that was her business. If she was feeling the person like that then so be it, and if the nigga didn't want her for that reason then it would be his loss.

Next, Omar had to tell Kayla who cried like a baby because at first she thought this would be O's time to leave Lydia for her. But when she learned it was a third woman in his life, she felt as though he would never be hers. She had cried in Omar's arms explaining to him she didn't mind being number 2 because she had plans on one day becoming #1, but #3 was too much. She also learned that day she had contracted the STD. Omar didn't know how he would tell Lydia but he knew this was going to turn into a whole lot of bullshit when he broke the news. But it had to be done. He just needed to send the kids to their grandma's house and sit her down and just do what had to be done.

Omar then came up with an even better plan, he just decided to call her on his way back home and just do it over the phone. Once the cat was out of the bag Lydia flipped the fuck out calling him all types of no good motherfuckers and hung up swearing. She was done with O she figured. She would just take the money she'd been saving and move on with her life. She had been feeling like Omar didn't think she was sexy enough for him, ever since their second child was born, which really hurt her. But to give her a fucking disease was the last straw and she couldn't even call her girl friends because she was too embarrassed. She just hoped the nigga hadn't gave her something worse. She made an appointment to see the doctor the following day.

Omar also felt dumb as shit. Here he was, getting too much money and now he was running around with a dirty dick hoping the medicine would have him cleaned up in a few more days. Knowing one of these bitches was looking him in his face, spending his bread and clowning him all at the same time really pissed him off. In his heart, he knew it had to be the newest addition to his stable; Sasha.

After letting her mom know she would be staying with her for a few days until she could find a place, Lydia cried like a baby for real. She was afraid of change and didn't have a clue how she could make it without this nigga she'd grown to depend on. She also knew in her heart it wasn't going to get any better if she stayed. She realized a long time ago Omar didn't want her as his woman anymore. She even thought about telling the feds all she knew but thought better of that for the sake of her kids, and the little hope she still held on to, that one day he would come to his senses and leave those nothing ass ho's alone in the street. If it wasn't too late for them.

Omar didn't know it but Lydia too had been playing phone games with a clown named Joe, she'd met through her home girl. He too was lightweight to blame for what little courage she had while making the decision to try to move out and move forward from this relationship that was only breaking her down. Joe was in her ear about how she could put Omar on child support and do better for herself like he was a better dude for her, but the truth being told he wasn't shit himself. He'd been trying to hustle his whole life and hadn't never amounted to shit. Every penny he made he gambled the shit up.

A lot of niggas didn't, and still don't, realize that habit was as bad as smoking crack. That's why he never took off and had resorted to trying to rob niggas and all kinds of broke ass nigga shit. But at the moment, accompanied by a constant late night rendezvous, and the dirty dick situation, Lydia had taken about all she could take and was going to give it a try.

Omar, not really wanting to see her face, just got a room and laid back for the rest of the night with his cell phone off.

CHAPTER 20

LOOK IN THE MIRROR

Coco was at Kayla's begging her to call Omar, which wasn't happening. O and Kayla had been fussing a lot and he was to the point of cutting her off as well.

Omar calling himself smart, called Kayla the day before and had her bring him four keys which he didn't even need. He just wanted to slowly get all his work out her house because he figured once she realized he was done with her she might do something stupid and fuck up some of his money he had left her. Omar had left her with only half a joint for when Coco was ready to make his move again. He knew it was about time for him to re-up. He knew it usually took about a week for him to get finished with his pack.

He felt bad about how shit had played out. In his heart he knew Kayla was a good chick. She just needed a good dude who was ready for a serious relationship. But he wasn't that dude. Because, for real, he had to conquer Sasha.

Little did Omar know but Kayla had a little friend herself that she had been fucking with for the past few months when he would be leaving her for dead. Hot and lonely for 3 and 4 weeks at a time she'd been careful with her choice though. She knew it was highly unlikely that they'd cross paths being that Ace was from Goldsboro, but had moved to ATL, and would just come back to Goldsboro to knock off e-pills and a little coke from time to time. He too, had begun to leave packs in Kayla's apartment for safe keeping while he was in town making his rounds.

Coco, getting desperate, had to get shit off today, because the impatient agents were on his back about getting Omar fucked up. They were starting to believe Coco hadn't been truthful with them; that he'd led them on. So, Coco figured he'd have to convince the agents to run down on Kayla's spot after he asked her for his package, which he knew Omar usually left with her for him. She told him to give her the money first, which Coco couldn't produce but he wasn't tripping, he just needed to know it was there.

Coco left Kayla's apartment telling her he would be back shortly with the re-up money. He rode a few blocks cussing himself for winding up in a position to where he would have to do some low down shit like that. And to make it worse Kayla was his first cousin and he knew she was there with her son.

As he placed the call to the agents, he almost hung up the phone. When he caught a glimpse of himself in his rearview mirror he felt so sucker at the time. He also knew after he placed this call he would never be able to attend anymore family gatherings. His moms would surely disown him because she loved her sister and for Coco to do some shit like that, it would truly put a serious strain on the two sisters relationship. But Coco felt like he couldn't do that time. Not taking into consideration he made the choice to live this life. It was the path he chose. Coco also had no regards for Kayla's small son but tried to make himself feel better about it by figuring Kayla wouldn't get no time. She would just have to give Omar up. As the agent answered the phone Coco explained to the agent that he couldn't get in touch with O, but that his girlfriend was his cousin and he knew for a fact that right at that very moment Omar had a serious load of stash at Kayla's apartment. He's seen it with his own eyes. Coco also stated that Kayla didn't know any better, that O was pretty much making her keep the work there.

The agent playing Coco, told him if this lead checked out it would be good. But since it wasn't a direct bust on Omar he still might have to do a little time. Coco couldn't believe his ears. He knew he'd been played. But it was too late now. He'd done spilled his beans. He wanted to know how much time. Still playing him, the agent told him he'd have to check with his boss. He assured Coco it would be alright, but he may have to make a few more busts in the near future to make all the time go away.

About 45 minutes later Kayla's door damn near flew off the hinges as the task force made their move. Kayla liked to had a heart attack as the agents stormed her living room as she laid on the floor playing with her son.

The agents were glad her son was present. Once they'd secured the apartment, the lead agent asked Kayla did she want her son to be placed in foster care. Or did she want to make the best decision for herself and her son right now. Because what was going on wasn't no joke and somebody was about to do some serious time. Before he could even finish, she was ready to cooperate. First the agent wanted to know where did she keep the drugs.

Handcuffed and crying like crazy, Kayla's words were barely audible, as she explained to the agents that the drugs were in her closet. Kayla's son cried loudly too, as he watch his mother crying, something he'd never seen her do.

While Coco rode around thinking who else he could knock off because he didn't plan on leaving his sorry ass baby's momma for one month, let alone some real time.

Once the agent found the key and a half and 400 e-pills, Kayla was allowed to call her moms to come get her son. She then learned she would have to ride with them downtown to make arrangements to make bail. Unless she could call Omar to come and get his shit out her house, so they could hide in the back room and grab him when he got there.

Kayla had to think quick and try her hand.

O was smart enough to sit her down on plenty occasions and explain to her the games these people played. He even lied to her about being caught up a few times and that he'd paid his way out of it. Being that Kayla thought that Omar was too rich, which he was doing real good, and the fact that Kayla had seen a few shows on TV where money always seemed to be the only way out, his stories seemed to be real. Plus she knew for a fact Ace didn't have money like O. So, she figured if she had to tell on somebody it would have to be Ace.

The agents were pissed when she told them that the shit didn't belong to Omar, which was partly true. The kilo and the 400 e-pills belonged to Ace. So, she just blamed it all on him.

The agent in charge stepped outside to call his supervisor to inform him that this fucking nigga, Omar had 9 lives. His supervisor couldn't believe his luck. He just knew he would be pad-locking his new home today, but told his agent that the other nigga would have to do for now and that they would send Coco's ass to prison for lying if he didn't do a few more busts of this magnitude.

Once back inside Kayla was told to call Ace to come over which she did, and as soon as he entered her apartment they jumped his ass and took him down. To make matters worse this fool had a Ruger P-89 on him plus about $15,000 in his truck. Ace couldn't believe he'd go out like that. He knew he wasn't hot. He'd been coming in town only dealing with his family. As far as he knew they were all good. The police weren't really on to them. He would have to wait to speak with a lawyer to find out how all this came about. Because unlike Coco, he had no intention of bring nobody else down because he'd fucked around and gotten caught up.

Once at the police station Kayla learned she still was being charged with maintaining a dwelling for the storage of the drugs. Plus possession with intent to distribute, which the agents informed her those charges would be dropped to a lesser charge as long as she continued to cooperate and she testified against Ace, if he decided to go to trial. Because so far he was claiming to know nothing about any drugs. The head agent also told Kayla, which was a lie, that he'd watched Omar coming and going from her apartment plenty of times and had witnesses who stated he had brought drugs to her apartment plenty of times.

Kayla admitted that her and Omar were in a relationship but he never allowed her to use drugs and that she had never seen O with any drugs.

The agent then said, 'if you called O right now and told him to come and get those drugs out your apartment what would he say?' Her reply was he's going to ask what in the hell I'm talking about and he's probably going to think I'm crazy because he don't have any drugs in my apartment. The agent said, 'Well, if you want to walk out of here right now, call him and say just that to him. Then we can be satisfied that those drugs belong to Ace. Because, to be honest with you, our reports are that those drugs belong to Omar. We never even heard of this guy Ace making any moves in this town.'

Kayla hated they'd boxed her in a corner like this, but she knew she had to make the call. She just hoped Omar would do like he'd been doing lately; that is, every time he saw a Goldsboro area code on his phone he wouldn't answer . . . that's why she'd started fucking with Ace in the first place.

Omar had gotten so bad about answering her calls that when she really needed him for bill money or something important she would have to drive all the way to Wilson and find a phone booth to call him from, with a Wilson number, so he would think it was one of his boys then he would answer the phone. Kayla would be like, 'damn-nigga you can't answer any Goldsboro numbers? But as soon as you see a Wilson number you answer that.' . . . Truly he hurt her and played a major role in her fucking around. She just hoped he was on his bullshit today. Because she truly didn't want to see him go to jail. Plus, she knew once he learned she'd went all out to save him, she would be rewarded highly, financially, and he maybe would consider her to be a soldier and a real ride or die chick.

Omar, still ducking Lydia's calls, didn't even have his cell phone on and Kayla's heart was able to beat again when Omar's phone went straight to voice mail all 5 times. The agents made her try again. They were pissed and just set bail for Kayla at $100,000, which she then began again to cry like a baby.

She thought she would be allowed to leave there, but there was no way in hell her mother would be able to get her. Once she was placed in a holding tank she got in touch with her mom who called Omar on 3 way several times for Kayla leaving him voice mail after voice mail.

The following morning when Omar woke up his phone was beeping repeatedly letting him know he had several voice mails, which he figured were all Lydia wanting to fuss, which was true with the first five. Lydia asked Omar over and over why he'd done that to her and what if he'd given her AIDS? Also she told O she was out of his house and that he was a coward for not answering his phone and he was a real weak nigga for letting a bitch come between him and his kids. Which Omar knew was right.

Then Omar's heart skipped a beat when he heard Kayla's mom telling him that Kayla was in jail on a $100,000 bail. O couldn't believe his ears then he knew shit was really real when the next voice mail was Kayla herself crying like shit telling him to please come and get her and that the other women in there were looking at her crazy. After hearing the many voice mails, he got in touch with his bail bondsman and had him get Kayla out ASAP. Omar also cursed himself for leaving his phone off all night, hating the fact that he hadn't been able to get her as soon as the shit went down because he figured the longer she was there the more questions she could answer. Plus, Omar wanted to know what the fuck had happened, but Kayla's mom didn't have any information for him other than the day before Kayla had called to get her little boy because she had to go downtown with the police because they'd found some drugs and those pills in her apartment.

Omar was like, 'Pills? What pills?'

Her mom didn't understand why he seemed so shocked. She hadn't ever seen Omar with drugs and she didn't have a clue that he was keeping work in her child's apartment, but she knew by the cars he drove and jewelry he wore that he was into drugs. So she automatically assumed the drugs belonged to him. She knew Omar gave Kayla plenty of money because Kayla didn't have a car or all the nice things she now had until Omar came into her life. O then asked, did Kayla tell you what they'd caught in her apartment and what came out of her mouth fucked Omar up. She said, I'm not sure but I think she said a kilo and a half, plus 400 pills.

Omar's mind raced like damn . . . was she stealing out my shit and making moves on the side? But he knew that couldn't have been the case because his shit was never short. Plus he didn't fuck with no e-pills period. O was ready to talk with Kayla because she had some explaining to do and he knew their relationship was definitely over, regardless of where that shit came from. Because his number one rule was when somebody in his circle got touched for dealing, especially with drugs, they were cut off.

CHAPTER 21

CLOCK TICKING

Omar had begun to spend a lot of time with Sasha. He really had nowhere to turn and he wasn't about to put no new people in his circle because it seemed every time he tried that, somebody would end up going to jail, and increasing his chances on going to jail.

He had spoken to Kayla when she got out and learned that she'd been holding work for some nigga named Ace. She broke down in tears. When O explained to her that no dope boy would trust some young chick with his product in her house unless they were fucking. She really had tried to stick to her story, but eventually told the truth; and blamed the sex on Omar leaving her for weeks at a time and her thinking O would never be hers.

With that news Omar was jive disappointed with little mama but chalked it up because he knew regardless of what happened with her and Ace, she wasn't going to ever be a part of his movement anymore anyway. He was also mad at himself for thinking with his Johnson and allowing her to convince him to hit the coward Coco off with work, because Kayla had told him how Coco had pretty much confirmed that she had some work in her apartment before he left. Then about 45 minutes later her door gets kicked in and now this nigga wasn't returning her phone calls.

Omar assured Kayla that she wasn't going to go to jail. He paid the $13,000 she needed for her lawyer. He had pretty much been ducking and avoiding her as much as possible blaming it on the police, saying they were following him and watching his every move.

O and Sasha were getting real close. In the meantime, spending everyday together because now he couldn't trust Kayla and she had moved up on the suspect list as one who could've given him that STD shit.

Lydia had moved in with her mom and Sasha had pulled out all the stops on locking Omar all the way down and pretty much cut all those trips out of town out. She also turned the sex game all the way up . . . brought this nigga breakfast in bed . . . the whole nine.

He was truly feeling himself. And it was a lot less headache being on some one-chick shit, he'd explained to Sasha, that if he came up with a dirty dick again, it was all on her because she was now the only woman in his life.

Sasha wasn't about to chance losing this balling ass nigga again. She reasoned she'd be a fool too. The nigga gave her everything she wanted and now he even had plenty of time for her. They traveled a lot in and out of Mexico, Jamaica and a few other islands. She was living out her dreams plus O got along well with her mother. What more could a girl ask for?

CHAPTER 22

THE PAST

Omar laid back reflecting on life. He had to wonder, had he chosen a good path in life? As long as he could remember this was what he wanted, but he knew people changed. He'd run into a few of his old classmates that had heard all the rumors about him, and truly looked up to him. But, he was proud of them as well. Even though he could never really see himself as being as square as a few of his former classmates. But, he had to admit that they were doing pretty good for themselves on the outside looking in. Not to mention a few of them bitches didn't look too bad either. But, none were as exotic as Sasha.

It seemed the more he matured the more he found himself thinking about who he once looked at as role models, and older dope boys that he used to swear one day he'd be twice as big as. The one called Nut from O's old hood had went down quick and had gotten 25 years.

He once thought he had a chance of being something in the game because at O's young age a few cars and a bad bitch seemed like that was what was up. Now that he was older he understood Nut was faking like shit and never even owned those cars, he was just making monthlies in another nigga's name and only lived in apartments throughout his whole little run.

It was true Nut had fucked some of the baddest bitches the game had to offer. But, what the fuck good was that? Omar knew Nut had been in for years. He'd heard Nut had even married one of those chicks that was too bad back in the days. But now she had kids by 2 or 3 different niggas.

Omar's other partner he used to fuck with hard when he was about 13 had been found shot dead after being involved in a gun battle with some other dope boys from another part of the city, over some bitch he'd slapped the shit out of, because she was mad he didn't want her no more because her home girl's pussy was better than hers was.

An older cat that the whole city loved, that Omar had never met, called Slim, who had a few blocks on smash back in the days was so major the police and all were on his payroll, and his outcome too, was all fucked up in O's eyes. Rumor had it that he'd gotten so rich the mob from NYC had him gunned down. The streets had too many stories about him. The story went that he was sitting on his own front porch playing with his grandson when the limo pulled up in broad daylight. When the back doors came open out jumped three crackers from the mob, all dressed in black suits, with pig masks on. They approached Slim, told him to put the baby down. Slim, seeing what it was, being that all the killers had their heat already drawn out, kissed his grandson and put him down and took those shots like the soldier he was. Even though it sounded gangster, it had to be painful to his family who obviously loved him, because it was very evident each year on his b-day his sons, who were now balling like crazy, were throwing a party the entire weekend to celebrate the life of the fallen kingpin, which Omar made it his business to attend each year. O respected how the old man's life was celebrated and respected his sons for how they put it down. The whole city was welcomed and the police didn't trip when the whole block was pretty much shut down for the whole weekend. No cars were even allowed to drive down the block on that weekend and everybody ate and drank all the steak and booze they wanted, on the house.

He really looked up to that shit. He remembered how the dope fiends and all couldn't wait for this weekend every year because they knew for a fact they would be eating and drinking for those days, nonstop. But sadly that too came to an end when the smarter one of the two sons got trapped off in some bullshit conspiracy one of his workers created on the block which ended up giving the brother 15 years behind those funky ass walls. The younger brother just wasn't the thinker the oldest one was and couldn't maintain without the other so that ship had pretty much sunk.

Omar had memories for days of fallen soldiers who either had told on a bunch of motherfuckers and was still doing a thousand years, or they'd been in the grave yard so long he'd damn near forgotten about them.

Breaking him from his thoughts, his cell phone was ringing. The voice on the other end really fucked O up. He wouldn't have guessed this if his life depended on it. It was that fucking Jamaican nigga, Slick, who'd been living in England the past few years and had blown through all that money he'd made in the '90s on one bad investment after another. Plus, he'd let his dick get the best of him as well, and that's why this phone call was on a 3-way from the county jail. Slick explained to O that he'd just been back in the States a few months, now, and had been in jail the whole time fighting a bullshit kidnapping case of his own son. Slick also told him that the name O was ringing so many bells in the county that he had to break down and reach out to his old homie. He also hoped they could leave the past in the past; which Omar didn't have a problem with. That, for one, he'd matured a lot since those days. Not to mention the fact that he couldn't give a fuck about Lydia no more, since two of his workers had called him telling him they'd seen Lydia going into an apartment with that bum ass nigga, Joe.

Slick asked him if he would get him out of that hole and he would explain to him everything that was going on with him. Which O didn't have a problem with doing, being that after all he had a lot of love for this nigga because back in the day, for real, Slick had put a lot of trust into him when he was a youngsta trying to find his way in the game. So, Omar figured if he could help the nigga, then why not? Plus, his bond was only $50,000; $5,000 with the bondsman. He figured, fuck it. For pennies he would free the nigga, if nothing else, just to hear what the clown had to say. He also wanted to know how he had fucked off a mansion in Miami, all kinds of Benzes and 740, to the point where you can't even come up with $5,000 punk ass dollars!

On the way to pick up Slick he thought about his partner who'd been killed by the same cat that had ratted on him. He too had had a hell of a run, but had been locked up for a bullshit case that the rat had basically put him on, and once he had beat the case the rat had shot the nigga to death and didn't get a day in jail for it. Taking all this into account, Omar wasn't sure if he was just getting older, or had fucked up on choosing his dream.

Omar pulled up at the barber shop on Nash Street where his man Mike worked, to meet Slick. He'd told Slick once O's bondsman, Mr.

Woodward, got him out to walk the one block to the barber shop, because Omar wasn't going down to the jail for nobody. Also, he figured Slick would need a haircut after sitting in the county jail for six months. When Omar arrived Slick was already there waiting.

Slick acted like he was truly glad to see O, and drove it home strong about how he always knew Omar would be a major playa one day. And how he was glad they could reunite after all these years. O was lightweight happy to see Slick, plus it felt good to be in the position where years ago he was working for this nigga and now the nigga needed him to post his bail. Omar thought it was crazy how the table could turn and you never know who you might need before it's over.

After they both got groomed up they headed out. Omar stopped by the mall to cop Slick a few outfits so he could appear presentable. Slick went on and on about how O was the man, and how niggas in jail was on Omar's dick. Slick also told him niggas wished they had some type of ties to O; once Slick had made that call to Omar and within 30 minutes Slick's name was being called to pack up. He asked him how he came up with his number and Slick told him some young cat had come in and heard him and a few other cats speaking on O, and the youngsta had said his girl had bought a car from him, and therefore had some paperwork with your contact info on it. So, he'd been lucky enough to come up with the digits. Slick also went on about he'd taken his son to England to get from this girl who'd caught him cheating and was doing a lot of bullshit around his son, which Omar figured that was Slick's story. He knew it was always two sides to every story. Slick explained to O that she had basically turned her back on him shortly after he stopped moving work in Wilson. Which made him think back to when Shorty used to come pick up Slick's money when Slick used to be O.T. She was absolutely beautiful but Omar respected the fact that this was the man's woman. So even though he wanted to say something to her bad, he played his position. At the time she was one of the baddest bitches he had ever come into contact with. He'd loved to pull out all his money to flash on her when she used to stop by his spot to pick up.

Omar had to snap back thinking about Shorty who had the prettiest eyes; but at the end of the day he was proud to say he never disrespected over no pussy, and that's why he was the one getting this weak nigga out of jail and paying for the nigga's outfits.

Slick and Omar stopped by K&W to grab a bite to eat, when Slick decided it was time to hit him with spill about how he had a few cats he could put on from back in the day that he felt were still loyal to his movement. He explained to Omar that he had a nice little chick to lay up with until he got back on; which he hoped it wouldn't be long, with his help.

After a few more hours of bullshitting around with Slick, Omar gave him the green light that he would fuck with him. After a few days passed he hit Slick with one key of raw powder and told him to bring back $24,000, which Slick was glad to hear, being that his boys had told him they would be glad to pay $7,000 for a quarter brick. At that rate Slick knew, with him not having any bad habits, he'd build up quick.

Omar continued to hit Slick with a brick every time he was ready for the next few months and had even knocked his price down to 22. Slick was moving fast, and like Omar, Slick loved motorcycles and had bought a brand new GXR1000, just like O's. Slick was feeling himself and thinking soon he'd be back strong enough to go to Miami and get some of his old Jamaican partners and wouldn't have to keep getting work from him. Because, for real, he appreciated everything Omar had done, but it still just didn't sit well with him having to get hit off by a nigga much younger than himself. Not to mention the fact this little nigga used to work for him. Slick didn't like the fact, too, that sometimes he felt like Omar was sunning him, too. Sometimes he would call and O would be busy and Slick would be put on hold for a few days until Omar made time to get at him.

A hard snow had hit causing Fernando to delay a drop off to Omar, leaving him with only 3 keys. O needed to cook 2 for his block and give a half to this chick who'd been down on his team for years. So Omar decided he would give Slick the last half of powder until he was able to see Fernando again.

Slick pulled up to O's spot a little sooner than Omar had anticipated and really didn't want Slick to see him in the process of cooking two bricks. Not that he thought Slick was a rat. It was just he didn't want cats to see his whip game. So, as he finished up what was in the pot when Slick arrived, he quickly gave Slick the half of a key and told him let that hold him a day or two, until the weather got a little better. Which Slick felt like was some son shit, not really respecting the fact that Omar had other cats to hit off.

Omar had been sensing Slick was feeling some type of way, but couldn't really trip on it because he knew at the end of the day he had to do what was in his own best interests.

He didn't know why Slick wasn't answering the phone. O brushed it off and figured he'd hear from Slick in a day or two. Little did he know, the night Slick left with the half a key of powder, in all that snow, he'd gotten into an accident and when the rookie cops arrived to assist they felt the need to search the car. Being that Slick's accent was so deep they automatically assumed he was a drug dealer. Slick, slipping, thinking because the weather was so bad, he could just put the work under the seat and slide back to his chick's house, got knocked with the half key and didn't call O because he knew from way back in the day he used to tell Omar if a nigga you fucking with gets popped, fall back from him point blank.

Omar told him his teaching was partly to blame for his long run in this game. O being so busy into what he was doing really didn't trip off not hearing from Slick in over a month. He just figured the nigga had run off with that little shit. Every time he called the phone it just rang until one day he tried the number and it had been cut off. So, he just chalked it up as a loss.

CHAPTER 23

SLOW DOWN

Omar pulled up to his homie Polo's apartment, who always kept some exotic weed to smoke on. Polo always called him when his brother got in a good batch. Polo's little brother was rolling good with the green and never entertained even fucking with coke but Polo had been moving coke with O for years.

Polo's girl Amy hated when Omar came around because she knew they would be gone half the day. Amy being young and madly in love really didn't have too many friends that she kicked it with, so she wanted to stick up under Polo all the time when she was home from college. Not to mention the fact that she didn't like Polo riding around with Omar in those fly ass whips he was always pushing.

Polo and Omar left the apartment to go do a little shopping. The two had been down so long they sometimes bought the same outfits just to stunt on other niggas around the city. After shopping and getting high for hours, O and Polo pulled up to the carry out drive thru to get a little something to munch on. That good ass green had them both too hungry, when out of nowhere Amy's Honda pulled up right beside them. She jumped out and opened Polo's door holding a large cup of grape soda in her hand and told Polo that if he did not get out of the car she was going to dash the whole cup of soda in his face. Before Polo could respond, O was like. 'man, you got to get the fuck out of here,' because he wasn't going for no soda in his Benz.

He was also tripping to himself because he'd never seen this side of Amy, even though he kind of figured she was a little wild the way she be acting sometimes. But he'd never seen her on this level, and by looking in her eyes O could tell she was dead serious. He wondered what the fuck Polo had been doing to this girl to have her tripping like that. He thought it couldn't be that much pussy eating in the world.

Omar told Polo again, 'man I'm going to catch up with you later.'

Polo said, 'Man, she be tripping like that sometimes,' and just jumped out of the car and ran.

He couldn't believe what he was witnessing. Omar didn't realize how fucked up shorty was. She didn't hesitate, she was right on that nigga's heels; left her car right there and all, still running. He later found out that's how shorty got down, and her sister was locked up for stabbing her boyfriend.

About two weeks later O gets a call from Polo's little brother saying he's got some new smoke in and that Polo had some for him to pick up. Omar headed straight for Polo's apartment and what he saw when he got there broke his heart. In front of Polo's apartment Task Force were in riot gear, the whole shit.

He kept it moving saying to himself he hoped that nigga wasn't dirty with no work. Omar knew from the past, plenty of times when he needed little shit for one of his little partners instead of running to the outskirts of the city, he'd just call, or stop by Polo's apartment, and grab a little 9 pack or something just to hold his workers down until he could hit them with something to really work with. O had told Polo on several occasions that he couldn't continue to sit up in that apartment, play those fucking video games, calling yourself hustling. He remembered plenty of times stopping by Polo's and this nigga would have a key of crack in the freezer while he was sitting back smoking weed with Amy and playing fucking Play Station. Omar stressed to him to put that shit in the woods or somewhere and take the chance on losing it instead of taking the chance on police running up in his shit praying that they don't look in the fucking refrigerator. O thought that was some real lazy shit. Omar rushed to the country wanting to hear something. He knew Polo had some work but didn't know if the nigga had taken his words seriously about not keeping that shit in that apartment.

About two hours passed before Omar got the call that he'd hoped wasn't coming. Polo's brother called saying Polo and his girl were down at the jail and needed 10gs apiece to get out, and that they'd been caught with four and a half ounces of crack cocaine in the refrigerator.

Omar was too pissed and swore that nigga Polo was going to give him his twenty stacks back, because he told that nigga too many times about that dumb shit.

Polo sitting in jail, knowing O was too pissed, was cursing himself for not taking Omar's advice. The scene kept playing back in his head how the whole shit had went down. It was Friday and sales were coming back to back for 8 balls and half ounces so he couldn't say who dropped a dime on him. But he knew one of those fools had to rat him out because he'd been taking niggas in the kitchen with him to grab the work and weighing it out on the freezer so he couldn't even say who the fuck told. But he knew it was one of them because the police hadn't even found the four ounces of weed he had had in his coat pocket in his bedroom closet. They went straight to the kitchen, opened the freezer and placed him and Amy under arrest.

The police were drilling Amy and telling her she was losing her scholarship if she didn't come up with something fast. When that didn't work, they tried to hit her with the fact that the apartment was in her momma's name, so they were going to have to lock her mom up. When Amy still didn't bite, the pigs were shocked. They were pretty much used to niggas telling on niggas with far less pressure than what they had already put on Amy. But Amy knew Omar had money and expected him to do the right thing, but told the agents to give her their card and if her man didn't take his charge then she would call them. The agents were cool with that. O didn't know they knew Polo was on his team. Omar called his bondsman's office and waited so he could speak with Polo. He also knew his bail bondsman could find out shit, sometimes.

Polo saw Omar sitting in the back of the bondsman's office . . . "Man you told me to stop putting that shit in the refrigerator!" . . . O just shook his head and thought about how many times he'd told Polo, "You can't sit around playing those video games, fucking your girl, all day, with that shit in the house, and the whole time you're serving motherfuckers from the spot . . . It's like you're a sitting duck and it wasn't if you get knocked, but it was when you get knocked."

Omar promised Amy and Polo that he was going to see them through this situation, and rolled out, knowing in the back of his head that he had to fall back.

Because he knew even if Polo went hard like he figured he would, he knew Amy was suspect.

Shorty was too wild, plus, she acted like she didn't want to make any eye contact with O while him and Polo discussed what happened prior to the raid and who he had been serving that day.

Omar had a lot of love for Polo and even though his bondsman told him a week after the arrest that they both had held their mouths, he still strung Polo along like he didn't have any work to give him yet, even though O had real love for the homie. He knew, being that Polo held his mouth that those people were still watching him.

Kayla had also been blowing O's phone up hitting him for 4 or 5 hundred here and there whenever she was able to catch him. And for real, even though Omar was in love with Sasha, he still craved a little taste of Kayla and was about to give in to those cravings. He figured it had been a few months since they knocked her and she hadn't been able to set him up or pinpoint any of his moves so the agents had focused on other shit that was going on in the city. So finally he told Kayla to meet him in Smithfield at the IHOP, so they could sit down and kick it. Just to catch up and O could feel her out a little and find out what her lawyer was saying. Plus, he knew by meeting her she would be down to take good care of him with a little of that top piece and that tight little juice box of hers. She'd been swearing to God to him that she hadn't been fucking around with anybody; which she wasn't lying. The dope boys from her city had heard about how she'd gotten knocked and that she'd set one kid up so they weren't trying to fuck with shorty at all. Omar had done fucked off $13,000 on a lawyer for her and was still pretty much her main source of income so after the meal they went to the Holiday Inn for some of what he had been missing, only to find out that there were no rooms available, so Omar was like "fuck it". He was so hell bent on getting up into those guts that he allowed her to follow him back to his house in Wilson, where they had a few drinks and he confessed to her that even though he was mad at her for fucking around, he'd still missed her much; which only made Kayla want to put it on him even that much more. She truly needed him back in her life because shit was real tight being that she might have to go another two or three weeks before she would be able to catch him for the little 3 or 4 hundred he would throw her way, just to hold her over.

So she just went on in for the kill, like her life depended on it, pushing Omar back on the bed she slowly undid his pants revealing a semi-erect penis, which wasn't a problem being that he had that juice in him. Plus, he'd popped a blue diamond (Viagra), while Kayla had walked to the restroom. She hit him with her slow no-hands head game, making his toes ball up like his feet were making a fist. She was so serious with that head game, before O knew it he was pushing her head back.

Little did Omar know that she had popped a Hall's winter-fresh cough drop in her mouth before she started topping him off, making the sensation almost unbearable. He hadn't been hip to that type of head ever in his life, so now he was back in love before she even began to straddle him with that tight ass juice box of hers. She began to ride him like he'd never been ridden before.

Kayla too was enjoying every minute of that hot sex, because for one, she was too happy to be on top of the bread winner. And the fact that he hadn't cum yet was even better she thought for sure he would've at least bust off once. But not tonight.

Omar was off on that pill dick so she was in for a serious ride. He watched in amazement as Kayla rode for about 10 minutes from the front and then she turned sideways and then she spun around a little more now with her back facing him. He was loving it. Then he stopped her and told her to give it to him from the back, he was so hype.

Kayla was putting in work and she wasn't like Sasha wasn't off the chain, but Kayla's pussy was by far the tightest between her, Sasha, and Lydia. After going in her deep from the back for about thirty minutes straight O finally busted off all in her and collapsed on the bed beside her and within minutes they were both sound asleep.

CHAPTER 24

IF IT AIN'T ONE THANG, IT'S ANOTHER

Omar rolled through, lost in thought, thinking about how he watched Kayla eating that dick. He knew he had to get her one more time, knowing he needed to leave her alone. Knowing that they could never have a future. He was snapped back to reality when his cell phone rang. Checking the caller ID he noticed it was Mr. Woodard, his number one bail bondsman, who told him he needed to stop by his office ASAP. So, O headed straight downtown to see what was up.

Once at the office, Omar waited while Mr. Woodard handled his business with a few clients. The wait was killing O, he knew this had to be some real shit for real, for Mr. Woodard to hit him like that. Plus, he knew having Mr. Woodard in his corner was truly a plus and Omar valued his words. Being that he knew the man, and had been using him as a bondsman since he was a shorty.

Once the office was clear Omar could tell by the look on Mr. Woodard's face that it was all bad, but he still held on to the hope that between the two of them whatever the problem was they could make it go away like they'd done so many times in the past.

Mr. Woodard, never being one to bullshit around with, now asked him if he knew a kid called Little J, which he felt instantly relieved, because he knew the cat, but had never dealt with him in any kind of way and couldn't even remember ever speaking to the nigga. But the sense of relief left him quick with what came out of Mr. Woodard's mouth next. He said, "you know he got busted in Virginia on 1-95 with $100,000 in cash."

Omar was like, "So, what the fuck does that have to do with me?"

Mr. Woodard went on to say that as soon as they knocked Little J that he began to tell them everything he knew. And though he knew the feds had followed Little J and a chick named Tina, that Omar also knew, who also happened to be related to Sasha, had went to meet a Jamaican cat that Tina had been fucking with for a little while, so she thought she knew the cat like that, but what she didn't know was this fool had been busted along with his mother and he'd been trying to get the charges against his mom dismissed and trying to get the best deal possible for himself. The Jamaican had heard Tina brag about her homeboy Little J who was supposed to be brick laying and decided to call her to see if she could make something happen. Being that she was from NC he figured by setting them up, that niggas in Richmond wouldn't know how he was getting down. So, Tina seeing an opportunity to make a few dollars, lied to Little J, saying she'd been fucking with this cat for this long and that his money was like that.

So Little J having all the sense figured fuck it, he'd make the move and Tina would be the one to serve the cat. So he should be cool if everything wasn't on the up and up. Everything seemed to be all love. Little J and Tina made the two hour drive to VA, and gave the Jamaican the 4 birds for the 100 racks and jumped back on 1-95. Everything seemed to be all good until they heard the helicopter sounding like it was damn near going to land on top of their car and the next thing Little J knew, blue lights were everywhere. Little J still holding on to the little hope he had left still figured he was cool . . . Tina had served the Jamaican, plus all they had now was money.

Once they were taken into custody Little J found out real quick that they weren't trying to hear that, 'I didn't serve nobody shit', and he too began to flip Tina who had already swore to God that Little J had made her serve the Jamaican which the Jamaican had already told the feds that Tina was just the middle man. So Little J did what he thought was the best thing to do under the circumstances and that was to try to put his fuck-up on somebody else's shoulders, not realizing that no matter what he told those fucking crackers his ass was going to the yard.

After many attempts to get Fernando's mechanic on the phone, Little J had no choice but to throw Omar under the bus - somebody who didn't have shit to do with him or his situation. He told agents that he knew that Fernando was the man, but that he had been dealing with Fernando's mechanic at Fernando's paint & body shop located in

Kenly, NC, but he also knew for sure that they could get the big man whose work they'd just purchased from him and Tina.

Little J was not giving any concern to O and his family. He wanted to know if Omar popped Fernando for them would they show some leniency to him for putting them on the right path, which he then learned they would have to ask their boss first since he made nothing happen directly.

After speaking with Mr. Woodward, Omar couldn't believe his ears and couldn't understand how this nigga Little J didn't even know him, for real, yet could do some ho ass shit like that. He also felt some kind of way about Fernando, even though he knew Slim was just trying to get his money. But the dude needed to understand how other nigga's actions bring heat to innocent motherfuckers who ain't got nothing to do with their slip ups. Omar was sick of hearing shit like that every time he turned around, another nigga was going to jail. He had to question if or when his number would be coming up and he decided he needed a vacation, so he got Sasha and hit 1-95 north and went up to D.C. to kick it with his family . . . just to get away from the bullshit.

Omar always came to the city to get away and he loved D.C. because he could do what he wanted and the police wasn't fucking with him. His cousin Little Pie, and shorty, always told him to leave that little ass town in NC and come back to the city to get money and he would be safe. He knew they would never rat on him. They'd been going hard for years and had a block that was cranking good in S.E. Every time he came up they always did it big.

Omar's aunts and uncles cooked big meals for him. Shorty and Pie would take him to all the clubs. His favorite spot was on Georgia Avenue, because it wasn't a big joint and you could really get up close and personal with the dancers. O had made it rain plenty of times in the joint so much so that he had to check one of the ho's one day when him and Sasha went out to Maryland to do a little shopping at Iverson's Mall and one of the dancers had recognized him from the previous night and couldn't resist the chance of making a play for the big spender. She tried to introduce herself pissing Sasha off real good. Omar liked how jealous Sasha would get over other chicks and he also loved how D.C. chicks go for what they want . . . that was something he liked about D.C. chicks.

Omar had to cut his vacation short when he got a phone call from his closest partner, T Money. T$, a real good nigga who had been rocking with O for years always made sure shit stayed in order for him when he would go out of town. He told O they needed to have a talk ASAP. Omar, knowing T$, knew that it was real important, because T was never on bullshit and had proved his loyalty a few times in the past. T was one of the only niggas in O's circle who'd been busted on a few occasions who could still deal with him on a hand to hand daily basis. T$ had been popped a few times in the last year or so and when money couldn't make it go away T$ would go lay it down a few years and come back home and get right back popping like that prison shit didn't even faze him one bit. So, him calling O like that made Omar know that something serious had to be up. He knew that he would have to wait and learn what was going on because they never fucked with the phones like that.

Once back in NC, T$ told O that a close friend of O's and T$'s had been popped with 9 ounces of crack . . . Rell was a cat Omar had also known for quite some time who he'd actually met through some beef when they were youngers; when he had his Honda scooter parked behind a chick's house one night who he had been fucking real good when Rell was walking home from a movie and noticed the scooter parked in the yard by a window. He figured he'd just come up on his ride home, plus something he could sell for a couple hundred dollars, not knowing the scooter belonged to O, even though he really didn't know O but he'd seen him a few times at school he had heard the rumors about O. Rell stole the scooter, pushing it up the street a few blocks before realizing he couldn't get it started . . . He'd left the scooter at one of his homeboy's houses.

Once Omar got out the pussy and climbed back out the window, he was too pissed to find his scooter wasn't there. He swore if he found out who stole his scooter, one of the last things his father bought for him before he started getting a little money that he would sure as hell try out his new .25 automatic on his ass!

It didn't take but a week before Omar had a name and the whereabouts of his scooter. Once he caught up with Rell he knew the kid looked familiar and found out he knew Rell's sister.

Rell, a little scared tried to play hard. Omar just slapped him a few times with his .25 and Rell quickly took him to his shit. After this Rell had been working for O ever since.

T$ explained to O that Rell had a partner in a town called Kinston, that he had been hitting with a little work, and a few days ago this friend called Rell and told him he was coming to Wilson to see him, which wasn't unusual. Rell knew his partner normally came to buy 4/2s on a regular basis. So, it wasn't nothing out of the ordinary. So, Rell hopped into his baby blue Mazda Millennium and headed to their designated meeting spot, which was the McDonalds located on 301 South in Wilson.

Rell, always watching his surroundings, took a once over glance of the parking lot. As he made his way into the parking lot he noticed his partner and a few other cars parked. Everything looked to be on the up and up until Rell noticed a white van with one white man in it. But when Rell attempted to get a closer look at the Caucasian, the white man quickly lifted his paper - lightweight sending red flags flying in Rell's head. But, being that Rell's pussy bill had been getting the best of him, being that he wasn't the cutest cat in the game, he'd been blowing money pretty fast to keep his new bitch happy, who had a mean head game and she knew exactly what to do with that tongue ring she sported. Going against his gut feeling that we all have when shit ain't right, Rell parked his car next to his customer's car. Rell really wasn't feeling comfortable.

Rell watched as his partner got out of his vehicle, keeping an eye on the mysterious man in the van. Rell popped the automatic lock, allowing his man to get in and told him they would circle the block right quick because Rell really wasn't feeling comfortable. No sooner had Rell backed out of his parking space he noticed the city's jump-out boys pulling into the McDonalds parking lot heading right in his direction. And in order for him to be able to make his getaway, he had to bump the jump-boy's cars with the front of his car. He sped out of the parking lot. Rell, now feeling like this nigga was on some bullshit.

He was begging to hit the panic and little did Rell know but the bump had busted his radiator and before long his car would be overheating.

Rell noticing his car was smoking lightly from under the hood, knew he had to get the work out of the car ASAP. So, checking his rear view mirror, he felt the little distance he had on the jump-boys might be just enough for him to bend a corner and toss the work, because he knew his run game was fucked up, being that all he did was eat all he could hold, not to mention the fact that he chain smoked Newports all day, every day. Rell reached under his seat and grabbed the 4 and a half began to roll down the window, all the while trying to keep an eye on the cops.

When he felt as though the coast was clear for a brief second Rell attempted to throw the work, when out of nowhere, the fucking informer knocked the work away from Rell's hand in an attempt to keep the work in the car, which really fucked Rell up. He now knew for sure this nigga was on some cold bullshit.

Rell, trying to keep the car on the road and punch the nigga in the face at the same time had to try to bend another corner and get the work out of the car - this time he managed to throw the work. Rell made it a few more blocks before his motor began to knock loudly, being that all the water had now drained out from the radiator.

Rell was going on his so-called man who said some weak shit about how they were trying to give him life if he didn't set some people up.

Hoping the pigs wouldn't be able to find the work, Rell pulled the car over, which had all but stalled all the way out anyway, as the cops ran to his car with their guns drawn snatching Rell and his partner, faking like his passenger, was being arrested too, they placed them in separate vehicles.

About ten more cops arrived on the scene. They all began to walk up and down the street searching for the work being that they knew he'd thrown it, from their informant.

It wasn't long before they found the pack and took Rell to jail, which T$ said Rell had quickly made bail. T$ told O he hated to have called him with that bullshit but wanted to let him know off the break what was going on and he needed to know how Omar planned on moving forward with Rell, being that Rell had actually been on his team for a long period of time, which Rell often threw in nigga's faces when shit wasn't going as he felt it should.

Omar hated the fact that niggas on his squad were getting fucked off like that lately, and all he kept hearing in his head was what Mr. Woodward had told him the agent said, which was the statements against him were building up fast. Whatever the fuck that meant. Omar not really being hip to how the feds got down thought in his mind that he didn't give a fuck about no statements. He felt as though as long as he didn't get caught with no work that a good lawyer would eat the case. Omar, also feeling tired of all this cat and mouse shit was beginning to feel like so many other cats in the game did and began to think the same silly ass way, saying to himself, fuck it, I'm in so deep, I'm just going to ball till I fall, which was some real dumb ass shit, knowing to himself that for real it was time to fall back, which he just couldn't seem to do. He attempted to fall back a few years earlier and couldn't stand it with his phone not blowing up every five minutes. Life was boring as hell to Omar. Plus his boys were crying like shit asking him when was he coming back to the game because they couldn't maintain their bills. O, feeling sorry for them and missing the game, came back in after only a six month break.

Omar put Rell on ice for a few months telling him that he felt as though the police were watching him. Which Rell knew was some bullshit, because he'd seen O cut niggas off plenty times before, in the past, for the same reason he was giving Rell the runaround right now.

Rell also knew Omar wasn't chilling for a while, like he kept telling him to, because Rell knew damn near everybody who worked for O and he knew for a fact that they were still getting money.

To keep Rell at bay O would pay his bills every month and had given Rell a nice 4-runner to drive while he waited on the outcome of his court case.

Omar had Sasha in his ear as well, telling him to leave niggas alone and that he didn't need that shit because he had everything he needed from the game already and his car business was doing pretty good and had the potential to do a lot better if he would take the time to really run his business and stop putting so much time into slinging all that shit in the hood.

CHAPTER 25

FEEL IT IN THE AIR

Growing tired of O giving Rell the runaround the feds came up with another plan for Rell to come at Omar with. They drew up some bullshit paperwork saying that Rell had signed a plea for 6 months for the charge of fleeing to elude and for damage to government property. With that paperwork Rell was now pressing for Omar to put him back into the game. Rell could tell the paperwork had O about to bite. Little did Omar know that Rell now really didn't like him too good. He felt like O had been playing him like a bitch. So he attempted to sell that theory to himself for the ho shit he was doing by becoming an informant, but for real in the back of his mind he knew he was telling because he couldn't sleep at night thinking somebody was going to get that no good ass bitch when he went to prison. So, for that alone O had to go.

Rell had even told people that O was pressing him to go to Kinston to kill the cat that had set him up. Omar had a few cats in Kinston that knew the guy who'd gotten Rell jammed up, and had gotten him the address to the nigga's baby momma's apartment. They had been laying on the nigga and pretty much knew when he came and went. He could've been took him down, but he wanted Rell to do it so he could feel like Rell was really down for his crime. And to let O know that he felt the same way about niggas working for the same people who fucked so many people's lives off for next to nothing, for so many years in the past.

Rell didn't understand that O truly did have love for him and hated the fact that he'd been caught slipping like that. Omar had even spared the nigga's bitch.

Rell didn't have a clue that one day his girl had seen him standing out front at his car lot and being the ho she was, she thought O was like most niggas and decided to try her hand. She hoped that once he got a shot of that hot pussy she would move on up the ladder and could cut Rell's ass off. So thinking she was looking too good to resist that day with the tight body dress revealing all her curves with the ass too phatt of the butt shots. She pulled into the car lot's parking lot and quickly jumped out, making sure O got a good view of that ass. She turned around and bent down to reach across the seat to retrieve her purse, which she had no need for, but knew he had to be watching that big old ass . . . so she put a little extra on it and took her time turning back around.

Omar was enjoying the show but was already on alarm because, for real, he didn't know what she had on her mind. He had been to their home on several occasions, but had only spoken to shorty briefly because Rell always escorted him to the back room to keep O's eyes off of her: being that he was insecure. Omar thought maybe she had some bad news or something because she'd never been in his presence without Rell being around.

Those thoughts quickly changed once she approached O with a big old smile on her face talking about, 'Mr. Johnson', she said, "Can we talk woman to man, between me and you only, with this conversation being kept top secret?"

His reply was, "Sure, why wouldn't we be able to talk?"

She then got straight to the point. O had to admit shorty was killing that dress and was jive sexy with her aggressiveness. She explained to him that she had a lot of love for Rell but she was a woman that wanted what she wanted and felt like she wouldn't get what she wanted unless she went for it. She said she wanted to suck every inch of his body since the first day she laid eyes on him.

He laughed and truly wanted to take her up on her offer, but knew he couldn't handle his little man like that. Plus, he knew how much the nigga loved this nothing-ass bitch. So, to keep shit at peace, he just played her to the left and gave her what she wanted to hear and was like, "For real, shorty, you bad as shit. Give me your number and I'll get at you."

She knew he couldn't possibly turn down the offer for some of that phatt ol' ass and left his car lot with a big smile on her face.

Omar had no intention of ever calling her. He just knew for sure that Rell was being played. Just like he thought when he first seen shorty with Rell. He called T$ and told him stop by the car lot, which T$ did. O told him to go ahead and put the nigga back down with a little something so he could stop crying about niggas not doing him right. He figured that bitch was running around on that bullshit, because Rell's money was a little funny these past few months.

Him, knowing how weak this nigga was, figured he might do something stupid like get to fucking with the police if he didn't hurry up and hit the nigga off just to support that ho's spending habits.

Little did Omar know that fool had done been sold his soul to the feds and had even pulled a robbery with his bum-ass cousin, trying to get some money for that no good ass bitch.

CHAPTER 26

IT IS WHAT IT IS

Rell was back on now. He caught himself playing two sides. He figured now that he was back in good with the team that he could make some money to stash away because he knew after he brought O down that shit would be tight for a while until he could find him a new plug. Plus, he knew whoever he started to deal with they wouldn't be just throwing him work like Omar was and that his money would have to be paid up front. This nigga really thought he had all the sense.

Omar was starting to get calls from Polo's girl because Polo was so fed up that he had refused to keep begging O to put him back in the game and the little shit he was buying from different hustlers in the city was a far different flip from when he had O throwing him whatever he needed. He agreed to meet with Polo's girl to try to feel her out because he didn't know what type of shit she was on.

They met at the K&W at the mall because he figured if this bitch is wired, with all the noise inside the restaurant, his voice may not get picked up, even though he knew he wasn't going to say no dumb shit out of his mouth anyway.

She explained to him that Polo didn't want to keep calling him because his pride wouldn't let him. Plus, she swore on her life that Polo would never tell and that he had already explained to her that the game brings good times and bad times, too. He'd also told her to prepare for him to go to prison because he wasn't going to tell shit and that once their court dates came he was going to take the blame for everything, freeing her all the way up.

Omar felt kind of bad because he knew his little partner was a soldier. But, O being so down for his crime, was just calling himself playing by the rules he'd set forth for himself and his family. But after a little consideration for Polo, he had played it off to Amy . . . like he'd been meaning to hit Polo off with some work but he really hadn't had it at the time when Polo had called. Omar assured her in the next day or two that Polo would be all the way back in the game and that he was going to stand by him all the way through this court shit and that he would spend his last dime trying to make sure Polo got as little time as possible.

With that being said, he made his exit from the restaurant without finishing his meal. When he noticed the nigga he'd killed all those years ago, baby's momma . . . the feeling he got when he saw the nigga's son was jive fucked up but he knew he couldn't bring the nigga back, so he kept moving towards the exit. Omar also couldn't help but notice that baby momma had done got thick as a motherfucker since the last time he'd seen her. He thought to himself that it was crazy for what he was thinking but little did he know that shorty really didn't place the blame on him completely, she had always felt as though Tatiana had been fucking Tone and Omar had shot him because he'd found out which was pretty much how the streets felt about the whole scenario, which was far from the truth . . . but once a rumor is out there, it's hard to convince the niggas who already pretty much think they know.

Once her's and O's eyes locked, she motioned for him to come over to her for a brief chat, which he reluctantly did. So after some small talk she told him that this wasn't the place but she really needed to sit down and talk with him. So, he agreed on a time to stop by her place, which he happened to know exactly where she was living because one of his partners lived in the same building. Omar left wondering was he tripping? But the vibe he got was like shorty was trying to get at him or maybe to cut into him for a few dollars for Tone's son. He knew in his heart that he didn't mean to kill the nigga, but knowing that wasn't going to bring back little Tone's father. So he made a mental note to make sure he had a few dollars on him the next day when he stopped by little momma's apartment.

Omar couldn't believe his eyes the next day when no sooner than he'd entered little momma's apartment before he could sit down at all she just started to unbutton her shirt dropping one piece of clothing after the next. He didn't know she had always wanted to fuck him when him and Tone were partners and she always said one day she was going to pay Tatiana back for fucking Tone and it didn't hurt in her eyes that O was too paid. She had heard about how well he treated his girlfriends and for real she could use a little help so this move was truly a win-win situation in her eyes.

Omar began to take his shirt off as well. When he seen how good that body was looking, thinking to himself, that he knew this bitch wasn't crazy enough to try to set him up or no shit like that and his manhood couldn't be feeling no fear either because it was pretty much already in go mode.

He couldn't believe how good that pussy was and had been by a few times to get up in that juice box. What had him fucked up was how loud that pussy got when he was hitting it! It was like she got so wet with each stroke that you could hear all types of gushy noise as he went in and out of her but the vibe went sour one day when he had stopped by for a quick taste and she had little Tone asleep on the same bed . . . as Omar was digging her back out. Once he reached his climax he thought shorty was some shit, for real, for having a dude's son there while she fucked the nigga who downed his father. That truly turned O off even though he wanted to feel like shorty was just trying to better her current situation.

Once he left he promised himself that he wasn't going up in little momma any more.

CHAPTER 27

TEMPERATURE RISING

The agent searched Rell's SUV while the other agent secured the recording device on Rell's body, making sure the mic was in a good spot so if Omar grew suspicious he wouldn't be able to feel it if he gave Rell a quick pat down or anything. Rell had told them that O had patted him down a few times lately like he was playing with him, but Rell said he felt like O was serious. Rell was lying to the agents trying to buy some time because they thought he was about to pick up some work from Omar, which was far from the truth. Omar had already told Rell that T$, O's man, was going to hit him off. But the agents, being so thirsty for Omar, told Rell to go pick the work up thinking it was coming from his hands directly.

Although Rell knew it was getting time to show and prove the feds were going to realize he wasn't trying to see this fool directly. Plus, the Mexican Rell and his cousin had robbed was putting word on the streets everywhere that he would pay good money for the name of the two fools who'd robbed him, which the Mexican wasn't tripping off the $27,000 and the key of powder they'd took. He just was fucked up about the fact that these clowns had tied up and raped his wife in front of him, after he had given them everything he had in the house at the time when they ran in on him. Rell knew his cousin had been running his mouth. So, he didn't know how long he had before he had to deal with that situation.

After coming back with the 9 ounces of crack the agents were happy, briefly, until they learned that the work hadn't come from O and that his voice wasn't anywhere near being on that tape. The head agent was so pissed off that he told Rell the next time if the shit didn't come directly from Omar, then the deal was off and he would just snatch T$ up and give him the same opportunity that they'd give to Rell. And that Rell's time-cut would have to be far less than what it would've been if he'd made the pick-up from Omar's hands directly.

Rell's eyes got big as shit. He knew he had to think fast 'cause there was no way in hell he was trying to leave that nothing ass bitch. So, O had to go one way or the other.

Rell couldn't sleep much at all that night trying to come up with a plan. He didn't know what else to do. He'd done showed Omar the bullshit paperwork the agent had given him to show O, stating the drug charges against him had been dropped which didn't make Omar deal with him directly. Then it hit him, he would have to create some problem with him and T$ so that way maybe then he could get to O which he knew was going to take some hell of an acting skill. But he figured in this stage of the game what else could he do?

Omar got a call from Rell; Rell was all loud talking about he was going to kill T$ and all types of shit. O had to make him calm down. He wanted to know what the fuck was going on with him and T$. Rell explained to him that his girl had been crying for at least an hour, talking about T$ had come on to her and had told her that Rell was going to jail for a long ass time and that she might as well get with him because Rell was finished and how O didn't even want to deal with him.

He couldn't believe his ears. Omar knew that he was no good and figured she may have come on to T$ the same way she came on to him and T$ must have taken the bait and told her how him and O really felt. Omar told Rell to be cool for a minute and he would call him right back.

Omar quickly called T$, asking him why you would try to fuck that nigga's bitch right now when you already know this nigga is weak for that ho . . . and might be ready to tell something?

T$ was dumbfounded. Like he didn't have a clue what O was talking about and swore on his kids that he hadn't disrespected that man like that and told Omar he would tell the nigga in his face, and that bitch, too.

Omar didn't know what was going on. But he knew that T$ was his man and believed if he'd moved on that bitch he would tell him. He also knew that the bitch was on some slick shit, too. So Omar had T$ meet him at their spot, and then called Rell and had him come to the spot as well, hoping they would be able to get to the bottom of this bullshit.

Once at the spot Rell knew he had to put on an Oscar winning performance. So, he laid it on real heavy from the moment he parked his truck. Rell hopped out on straight bullshit, running up on T$ like he really wanted drama. Omar had to jump in between the two to keep them from fighting. O tried to explain to them that they'd been down too long to be letting anybody come between them and that they should be able to talk about whatever problem they had with one another like men instead of fussing back and forth like bitches.

T$ continued to swear on everything he loved that he didn't have a clue what this fool was talking about. He swore he would never cross that line on that man.

Rell truly deserved an Oscar, because he kept faking like shit until O was just like: 'nigga, roll out. When you need something just call me and I'll handle it' . . . cause Rell had swore that he was going to kill T$ for trying him like that and that T$ better not ever call his phone again for nothing.

Once Rell heard what he wanted to hear, he jumped back into his truck satisfied that his mission was completed.

CHAPTER 28

WHEN IT ALL FALLS DOWN

About a week later Rell called Omar telling him one of his good men was ready to re-up on his weekly 4 and a half. Rell, having all the sense, told him it was a cat from Raleigh that he knew. O was pretty cool with the name, Unique, but questioned to himself why Unique hadn't called him direct, because unbeknownst to Rell, Unique had been dealing with O from time to time without Rell's knowledge, even though Unique was Rell's worker who'd only met Omar after Rell had brought Unique to O's car lot to buy a van for his baby momma. Omar really didn't trip though, and just figured Unique had been in town just kicking it with Rell. He knew that he often came into town just to hang with Rell, so he really didn't give it a whole lot of thought since Rell and Unique had become close in state prison. O told Rell to meet at the spot.

Rell, following the agents instructions, who was geeked up thinking he was getting real close to getting his man, told Rell to tell him that it needed to be quick, because Unique needed to hurry back to Raleigh to pick up his kids from day care because Unique's car was getting painted so he had driven his baby momma's van down to Wilson to score the work. So he was waiting for Rell to bring the work back to the Bojangles on 264.

O, having kids himself, got right on it, being that he often times had to put his kids in the middle of that drug shit trying to get that almighty dollar.

Agent Brown made sure the wire was in place and sent his crash dummy, Rell, on his way.

Omar jumped in Sasha's truck, being that they planned to do a little grocery shopping after the meeting with Rell at the spot. Which, at the time, Sasha didn't know who he was going to meet. Which she couldn't have cared less. She was just happy that O was spending his day with her. She had begun to feel like his eyes were beginning to wander. And she started asking O, 'was he fucking, out of his mind', when she saw Rell's truck parked at the spot. She'd heard him, so many times, say that he couldn't fuck with no nigga after he's been arrested for drugs. That was his main rule and the reason for his longevity in the game. So she wanted to know why he'd chosen to cross the line. Also, she had noticed that lately he'd been doing the same thing by dealing with Polo. She was like, "damn nigga, you got plenty of money, why are you fucking with these niggas, still?"

Omar knew she was right, but still hopped out of the truck and gave that fool the work.

Once Rell had the work he said what the agent had told him he must say, which was "how much you want for this?" which O knew right away that the shit wasn't right because this nigga had been getting work from him at least for the last 5 years and he knew damn well Omar got $2700 for the 4 and a half so he didn't even say, shit he just smiled and knew he'd done the right thing by bagging the 4 and a half with gloves on and put an extra bag on top of the plastic bag that the work was in so that when he passed it to Rell he made sure to keep the plastic bag that was on top which was the only one that had his fingerprints on it. Backing away from Rell's truck with a smile on his face, Omar just put his hand to his face in a motion like I'm going to call you and turned around and walked away without ever saying shit to that nigga just in case he was wired.

Omar thought to himself when he got back into Sasha's truck that he knew now for sure that he would never give this nigga any more work.

Sasha, shaking her head, was too mad at him, saying she had a bad feeling about that nigga, Rell.

Omar didn't say much because he felt like that nigga was fucked up. But still, he hoped it was his own paranoia that had him tripping. But deep down in his gut he knew every man and woman is equipped with that sixth sense that lets them know when something's just not right and he knew you couldn't ignore that warning.

After bending a corner or two Omar felt like he was being followed so this too had Sasha going crazy. Him being the quick thinker that he was, he drove to the Honda dealership where he had a little Honda Civic getting a tune-up. He drove all the way into the work area of the Honda shop and went inside telling Sasha to drive off and go to Wilson Tech College where she was enrolled taking some accounting classes and that he would call her shortly. As Shasa exited the Honda Shop the unknown car began to follow Sasha's truck again, not knowing that he had made his escape.

Twenty minutes later Omar pulled outside in the Honda and headed straight to Raleigh to his apartment that he had on the low that not even Sasha knew the location to.

Rell called O a few days later asking if Omar could meet him on the spot. The agents were pissed that his voice wasn't on the tape. They were also waiting to see if the fingerprints found on the plastic bag the crack was in had any good prints on them from Mr. Johnson. Omar was real short with Rell giving Rell that feeling like he'd been made.

Polo, on the other hand, had worked his way back into O's good graces.

CHAPTER 29

I NEED A VACATION

All Star game 2003, in ATL. Omar, T$ and his man Polo and the homey Greg were getting ready to hit 85 South. He hadn't spoken to Rell in over a month. O was thinking he would see what the vibe would be once the two came into each other's presence. The All Star game was something the crew did annually.

Omar called Rell's cell phone which went straight to voice mail on 4 or 5 different tries. So he told the boys they would just go ahead and hit the road. They figured Rell would show up or just meet them in ATL. The funny thing was that no one in the crew had recalled the last time they'd seen him; not that any of them were really looking for him, but now that they thought about it, they all agreed that it had to have been at least a month since anyone of them could recall seeing the nigga.

Once in the A, the crew checked into their rooms, got dressed, and hit the parties. Bad chicks were everywhere, plus mad celebrities. Omar was working his magic on that one chick from the show 106, who he thought had to be the thickest chick in the A at the moment.

She could tell Omar had to be all the way on, being that the boy had on at least $250,000 on his neck plus like 50K in his mouth. The only thing that had the mood a little off for O was the fact that the boy Rell still wasn't answering his phone. He even tried calling Rell's sister, who claimed that she didn't even have a clue where this fool was at, which Omar found to be very odd. He brushed it off thinking he'll just track him down once he made it back to the city.

A few days after they got back in town Omar got a call from T$ telling him it was important and that he needed for him to meet him right away because he had a letter from the nigga, Rell.

Omar was like, "a letter? Why the fuck would he write you a letter?"

T$'s reply made him almost drop his phone; the nigga had sent T$ the letter from FCI Beckley, a Federal prison in Beaver, West Virginia. Omar couldn't believe his ears. He also had the feeling in his gut that he really didn't like. A feeling that made him feel as though everything was all bad. He rushed to T$'s apartment to read the kite.

All types of shit raced through Omar's head, as he made the drive to T$'s apartment. He kept checking his rearview mirror thinking he was about to be pulled over at any minute. Once at T$'s, he got the kite and was fucked up by the kite's contents immediately ...

"Dear T$, man I'm so sorry how I came at you about ole girl. I was wrong as shit, but I was feeling shorty for real, but I know in my heart she's no good for me. Plus, like used cars we been down for too long for us to be tripping over some pussy. But, I'd fell weak. So, I'm sorry for coming at you like that for real and I know you're tripping over my new address, but I couldn't really tell you what was going on. I thought I was going to beat this shit. But, I'm cool that I only got 5 years, and I turned myself in about 2 months ago. But, yo, I just had to let you know how I was feeling and tell 'used cars' everything is cool. He ain't got to worry. So stay up homie and when you can, send me a few flicks . . . Rell.

Omar gave T$ back the kite knowing in his heart his days had to be numbered, but a little part of him hoped this fool spared him.

Six months passed and nothing happened. He had begun to feel like all was well. His spots were doing numbers and everything was good.

Omar got out of bed looking at Sasha, thinking he should get him a little morning sex, but thought 'fuck it, I'll bust her up when I get back today'. He had a whole lot of moves to make and had planned to get an early start on it. First, he stopped by his car lot and waited for his man Polo to stop by, who had a few G's for Omar to pick up. The two stood out front of the lot looking at some new smoke Polo's brother had just gotten in, when they noticed several different cars that had out of state tags.

Omar began to laugh and ask Polo if he'd been keeping up with his court dates. Polo had told O that his date had been postponed for two more months. With that being said, the two went their separate ways. Polo went north toward Rocky Mount while he went south, heading back into the city.

Omar noticed a car come up behind him moving a little too fast, so he figured he would just change lanes so this fool could keep pushing, since it seemed he was in rush. When the car changed lanes as well he took a closer look in his rearview mirror and noticed the pair in the car was one white and one black; which made him feel like these fools were police. Coming up on the stop light Omar decided to make a right to see if they continued to follow him. They too made a right on red, leading to Nash Street. After he traveled another block he noticed a white Yukon pull up beside him full of big crew cut having, police looking, motherfuckers, when about the same time the car that had been tailing them threw on the blue lights in the grill. Omar knew what it was for sure then. He knew he wasn't dirty, but knew this shit wasn't about no search shit. These people had them papers.

Omar pulled over, still hoping it wasn't over, with all types of shit running through his mind: like his kids, and the pussy of his getting gutted out by another nigga, and years behind those walls, if not the rest of his life.

He sat there with the doors locked looking straight ahead with all those thoughts running through his head, back to back . . . when he heard a banging.

The agents with the vests on that read FBI and DEA on the front and back .

Omar blinked his eyes several times as the banging continued. He felt a bit of cold air then realized his mom had pulled the cover off his body and was yelling at him to wake up! She'd been banging on his bedroom door because she wasn't giving him another ride to school, if he let the bus leave him again.

He quickly jumped up and looked around, thinking, . . .'Damn, that was a crazy ass dream he'd just had. Especially for a 13 year old kid.

Omar thought to himself, as he got dressed, that he hoped like hell he made it to the NBA or something because those dope boy thoughts he'd been having lately were out of the question because it was far too many rats in the game these days for him to throw his life away like that.